UP JUMPED THE DEVIL

BOOKS IN THE ARGOSY LIBRARY:

UP JUMPED THE DEVIL

CLEVE F. ADAMS

THE BROTHERS OF THE SNAKE: THE
COMPLETE CHINATOWN CASES OF
JIMMY WENTWORTH, VOLUME 3

SIDNEY HERSCHEL SMALL

A CLUE TO THE COPPER: THE COMPLETE
CASES OF SILVER SKULL

RICHARD HOWELLS WATKINS

KINGDOM OF THE LOST: THE ADVENTURES
OF PETER THE BRAZEN, VOLUME 8

LORING BRENT

WORTH MILLIONS

RICHARD BARRY

TIGER DICK'S DOUBLOONS

DON MCGREW

PRESIDENTS: IMAGINARY MOMENTS IN
THE LIVES OF AMERICA'S GREAT

THEODORE ROSCOE

CROSS OVER NINE

MAX BRAND

ASOKA'S ALIBI: THE COMPLETE
ADVENTURES OF BEN QUORN, VOLUME 2

TALBOT MUNDY

THE LOST PUNCH: THE COMPLETE CASES
OF GILLIAN HAZELTINE, VOLUME 4

GEORGE F. WORTS

UP JUMPED THE DEVIL

FROM THE CASEBOOK OF REX MCBRIDE

CLEVE F. ADAMS

INTRODUCTION BY
KARL SCHADOW

ILLUSTRATED BY
DAN CONTENT

COVER BY
RAFAEL DeSOTO

POPULAR PUBLICATIONS · 2025

TABLE OF CONTENTS

THE RADIO ESCAPADES
OF REX MCBRIDE

by Karl Schadow

AT THE CLOSE of this volume, Cleve F. Adams, in a 1945 version of a previous 1942 article noted a significant update concerning his most famous character: "(Rex McBride has sold to both pulp and slick magazines, to the movies, to radio)." The hard-boiled private investigator was introduced to readers in the 1938 issue of *Double Detective*. Subsequently, his exploits graced the pages of *Detective Fiction Weekly* were collected and published in novel form. *Up Jumped The Devil,* the subject of this volume had been published as both a novel and in *Cosmopolitan* (June 1943). And though Adams states that McBride has had movie offers, it is unknown if such a feature was ever produced. Adams is to be recognized, however, for his contributions to two motion pictures, *To Have and Have Not* (1944) and *The Fatal Witness* (1945). In *Cornucopia of Crime* (2010), Francis M. Nevins wrote a comprehensive chronicle of Adams career but with a limited account regarding those characters adapted to radio. Thus, the present study expands on the Nevins opus.

Though Rex McBride is the most well-known Adams

character, he was not the first to be transformed to radio. Private eye Bill Rye holds that honor when he solved "Murder Ad Lib" on *The Mollé Mystery Theatre* July 11, 1944. This weekly, half-hour anthology on NBC sponsored by the Sterling Drug Company offered the best of classic and modern stories in detective fiction. The Rye yarn had been adapted from the May 17, 1941 issue of *Detective Fiction Weekly*. Two months later on September 12th, another Adams creation, Police Lieutenant Connor O'Melveny made his sole appearance on the program in "Give the Guy Rope." This thriller was culled from the August 20, 1938 issue of the same magazine. Rex McBride would have been a natural addition to the radio series culminating in a trio for Adams, but another—Rex Sackler, created by D.L. Champion—was selected. The Sackler yarn was broadcast July 3, 1945.

It was not until the summer of 1946 that Rex McBride first thrilled the listening audience in "Backfire" broadcast July 14, 1946 on *Silver Theatre*. This weekly anthology of alternating comedies and dramas had been a staple on CBS for over a decade. Sponsored by the International Silver Company, the program's 1946 summer session was a fill in for the vacationing Ozzie Nelson family. The original tattered-page tale by Adams published in the November 30, 1940 issue of *Detective Fiction Weekly* was adapted by Carlton E. Morse, a widely acclaimed dramatist who had created for the etherwaves the highly successful *One Man's Family* and *I Love a Mystery*. In "Backfire," McBride is hired to retrieve $5,000 taken from a meek man by a swarthy swindling duo. Kay Ford, who is Rex's girlfriend in the McBride stories has an integral role and nearly gets herself

killed. Stage and screen actor Brian
Donlevy starred as McBride in the
Silver Theatre rendition. He was
an excellent choice having essayed
leading roles in several hard-boiled
films including *The Glass Key* (1942)
and *Nightmare* (1942). Unfortunately, the supporting cast in the

Frank Lovejoy

"Backfire" radio episode is unknown. Moreover, there is no
extant script nor audio of this particular broadcast.

It would be three more years until radio rediscovered
McBride when *The Hollywood Reporter* (May 24, 1949)
declared: "Frank Lovejoy in *Here Comes McBride* and
Edmond O'Brien in *Nightbeat* look set for NBC summer
airing." Auditions for both of these proposed series had
been recorded in NBC's Hollywood studios five days
earlier on May 19th. These trial recordings were expected
by the network brass to lead to regular weekly series. The
May 19th date is often misconstrued as an actual broadcast date of the episode which it is not. Whether or not
the audition was actually aired by NBC for the general
listening audience or close-circuit for network affiliates
only remains to be determined.

The *Here Comes McBride* project was directed by Warren
Lewis who had commenced his career in radio during the
late 1930s as a writer. After serving with the Army Air
Force during World War II he was employed at NBC in
various capacities leading to a promotion to the network's
production staff. Robert Ryf whose previous work in the
medium included several scripts for *The Whistler, Escape*
and *The New Adventures of Michael Shayne* was enlisted

by Lewis to transform the Adams thriller *Up Jumped The Devil*.

For the *McBride* audition, Frank Lovejoy was selected to portray the hard-boiled investigator. One of the finest actors in the industry, he had recently completed a two-year stint as Craig Rice's attorney, John J. Malone in the ABC series, *Murder and Mr. Malone*. Lovejoy had appeared in numerous radio programs both in Hollywood and previously in New York. His entertainment career was extensively profiled in a seminar at the 2021 Mid Atlantic Nostalgia Convention.

The plot of the thirty-minute radio play was of course condensed from the 200+ page novel. In molding the radio play from the original tome, Ryf retained the basic storyline with McBride finding himself in San Francisco searching for a stolen necklace. However, a brief introduction of three major supporting characters transpires in the airwaves iteration before McBride enters his hotel room and finds a dead man. He is then immediately accused by the local police of the man's murder. The action then accelerates with additional murders and mayhem. Warren, Ryf and Lovejoy all received on-air credit during the broadcast. In a gratifying gesture on the part of Warren Lewis, Adams was the benefit of oral curtsies both at the beginning and closing of the audition.

Though they were not acknowledged on-air nor in trade publicity, the supporting players have been identified. Joan Banks (the wife of Frank Lovejoy) portrayed the bookkeeper Susan Lee. During the story, she is courted by the Trojan Hotel's manager Mr. McGillicuddy played by Jay Novello. There is also romantic interest involving McBride and Lee. Excellent chemistry is choreographed between Lovejoy and Banks throughout this drama. Jack Petruzzi is Homicide Lieutenant Orsatti, frustrated by McBride's presence in the case. The use of Orsatti by Adams (and retained by Ryf) may be an inside joke as Lou Orsatti was then the president of his own talent and advertising agency. Had Adams been trying to negotiate a movie or radio contract of the McBride property with this firm upon the novel's original publication in 1943? Another tip-of-the-hat is the tribute to Raymond Chandler. The family from whom the necklace was stolen is named for the creator of Philip Marlowe. Mr. Chandler is played by Ted von Eltz. Both Petruzzi and von Eltz double as reporters during the beginning of the episode. Mrs. Chandler is played by Eleanor Audley. Lawrence Dobkin is the gambler Sean O'Hara with Paul Dubov as his henchman, Al. Dubov also doubles as the tobacco shop proprietor.

The music for *Here Comes McBride* commenced with a short segment of Wagner's "Here Comes the Bride" and then immediately transitioned to an ominous interlude prefaced by gunshots. The person at the organ console is unknown but is not the East Coast-based Henry Sylvern who has been incorrectly reported by print and online sources.

Here Comes McBride was certainly a priority for NBC as the network's President Niles Trammell alluded in an exclusive interview with Ben Gross, radio editor of the *New York Daily News*. In that column of June 19, 1949, Trammell revealed the names of several new radio series that the network was offering including *The Halls of Ivy*, *Gordo* (from the *Gus Arriola* comic strip) and *Night Beat* (noting Edmund Lowe instead of Edmond O'Brien) along with *Here Comes McBride*. Noteworthy is that none of these hit the air during the summer of 1949. Despite repeated attempts by NBC Sales Department, *Here Comes McBride* remained on the shelf. During the winter of 1949–1950, there were dispatches of continued efforts by the network. *The Hollywood Reporter* (December 30, 1949) remarked: "NBC cutting second audition of *Here Comes McBride* with Frank Lovejoy." One newspaper *(Los Angeles Examiner,* January 6, 1950) was enthusiastically optimistic of the series and its leading actor: "We hear Frank Lovejoy will shortly audition a new series, *Here Comes McBride,* on NBC. The radio actor made such a hit as Sergeant Mingo in *Home of the Brave* that he's being mentioned as an Academy potential." Alas, this second undertaking did not result in a dedicated series.

However, two print sources suggest that the program was on the air but during different seasons. Vincent Terrace, in his 1999 tome *(Radio Programs, 1924-1984)* cites the program as broadcast during the summer of 1949. *Radio Crime Fighters* (2005) authored by Jim Cox disclosed that the program entertained listeners during the spring of the same year. Neither source correctly states that the one extant episode was an audition. Moreover, Cox posits as a disputable reason the series did not achieve a favorable outcome: "McBride was an L.A. private insurance investigator (though in no way a threat to the popularity of contemporary *Johnny Dollar,* then airing over CBS)... Perhaps two private insurance investigators proved to be one too many." When NBC recorded and announced their *McBride* venture, *Johnny Dollar* had been off the CBS schedule following its April 22, 1949 session. It did not return until the following July 17th. Was NBC taking advantage of that program's absence to promote their own version of an insurance investigator? Upon his return in the role of Johnny Dollar, Charles Russell remained the headliner through January 14, 1950. The part was then acquired by Edmond O'Brien three weeks later on February 3rd. What had transpired regarding O'Brien and the *Night Beat* audition? This proposed series was also left on the shelf by NBC. However, upon the dissolution of *Here Comes McBride,* Frank Lovejoy successfully auditioned for *Night Beat.* This series commenced on NBC, February 6th, three days after O'Brien began his three-year stint on the rival web.

Based upon the audition, Frank Lovejoy would have been superb as Rex McBride. Had *Here Comes McBride** actually made it to the NBC schedule (either sponsored or as a sustainer) would *Night Beat* have progressed to its status as one of the medium's finest noir series? Another factor which may have inhibited the advancement of a *McBride* series was the death on December 28, 1949 of Cleve F. Adams. No archive of the author's career has been identified. Thus, it is unknown if negotiations for a radio series were continued with Vera his widow, or son, Warren.

---

* The audio of *Here Comes McBride* may be accessed at the following link https://archive.org/details/Singles_And_Doubles_Singles_H-K/49-05-19_xxx_Here_Comes_McBride.mp3

UP JUMPED THE DEVIL

1

MCBRIDE PAUSED JUST inside his door and regarded the dead man with some astonishment, for while this was not the first dead man he had ever seen it was certainly the first time he had found one sitting in his own room. Presently it occurred to him that it was not his own room, and he turned, opening the door a trifle wider, and compared the number on the door panel with that on the key he still had in his hand. No, he decided, the mistake was the dead man's, not his.

Further evidence that this was so was McBride's bag, a well-traveled but expensive Gladstone, on the luggage rack at the foot of the bed. It was on noting the bag that McBride's astonishment underwent a sudden metamorphosis and became a red, unseeing rage, because the Gladstone was his pride and joy, and someone—someone who hadn't taken the trouble to see if the bag were unlocked—had cut a slash in the leather big enough to drive a truck through.

With exaggerated calm McBride closed the door. Then, hands on hips and murder in his heart, he went over and planted his feet in front of the dead man. "You?"

The dead man returned McBride's stare with macabre intensity. Then, head rolling in a sort of stubborn denial that it had been he who profaned the bag, he sagged far over to one side and finally slid out of the chair and fell on his face. A little blood from his mouth dyed the tip of McBride's brown shoe an ugly purple. McBride looked down at the man's head, which was bald except for a fringe of reddish hair, and at the haft of the knife protruding from between the man's shoulder blades. Being a stranger in a strange town, he thought it might save trouble all around if he just put the dead man outside in the hall for the porter to find. But habit was strong within him and presently he went to the wall phone and lifted the receiver. "I want a policeman," he said. He remembered that the directions in the front of phone books said that was all you had to do.

A startled but very lovely voice said, "A—a policeman!"

"On second thought," McBride said, "you'd better make it two policemen." He hung up. He was a carefully dressed medium-tall man, very dark as to hair, eyes and skin, though the skin had none of the muddiness usually associated with dark complexions. He looked as though some of his Black Irish ancestors who had helped drive the Union Pacific through Sioux territory might have been on more than amicable terms with the female of the species. His eyes were faintly resentful and he was still very sore at whoever had slashed his bag, but as yet there was no fear in him; no presentiment that the murder of a strange man in his room was going to cause him, McBride, more than a slight inconvenience. He was very careful not to touch anything, not even the Gladstone, because that is the first question the coppers always ask you and he wanted to break clean and get on with the business of the Cyrus H.Q. Chandlers and the Adelphi necklace.

After a short interval he heard the decrepit elevator clank up and come to a creaking, protesting halt outside.

He opened the hall door. He was still wearing his hat but he took this off when he saw that his visitors were not cops. One was Mr. McGillicuddy, an unusually pale and palpitant little man for one who wore such a ferocious name. Mr. McGillicuddy managed the Hotel Trojan.

With him, and the real reason for McBride's taking off his hat, was a very beautiful girl indeed. Obviously she was some sort of employee, because she was wearing black sateen sleevelets to protect the cuffs of her white satin blouse. Also she had a pencil in her hair. But even with the tremendous handicap of the sleevelets and the pencil she was still something to look at. Her hair was a rich coppery brown, and her eyes were brown too, intelligent but warm-looking. McBride thought that probably the nice voice he had heard over the telephone belonged to her, and this impression was immediately confirmed: "What's wrong, Mr. McBride? Why did you want a policeman?"

McGillicuddy said nothing at all. His mouth kept opening and closing, like a gasping fish, but no sound came out. His eyes were wide and pale and frightened behind thick lenses.

McBride stood aside and waved a hand at the dead man on the floor. "Wouldn't you want a policeman?"

"Oh, my God!" Mr. McGillicuddy said. It was almost like a sigh. He quietly folded up and sank to the floor in a dead faint.

The girl, however, was made of sterner stuff. She went very white and her two small hands clenched into fists, but she did not faint. "Why—why, that's Mr. Severn in 514!"

"He isn't in 514 now," McBride pointed out. "He's in 414. That's what I wanted to see the policeman about."

The full impact of it hit her then; the knife and the blood and McBride's apparent callousness. One hand went to her mouth and her eyes met McBride's with a horrified stare. "Oh!" she gasped. "Oh, how could you?"

"How could I what?"

She retreated from him. "How can you stand there and look so smug and self-satisfied when a man is—" Her eyes grew very wide indeed now and she started forward. "Why, perhaps he isn't dead yet!"

McBride caught her by the arm. "He's dead, sister, take my word for it. I've never seen anyone any deader. You call the cops like I told you?"

She shook him off. "Of course. But Mr. McGillicuddy said— Oh, poor Mr. McGillicuddy!" She dropped to her knees beside the stricken manager. "Water!" she commanded McBride fiercely. "Get me some water!"

"Not me," McBride said. "I've already touched the doorknob and the light switch and the telephone. That's enough."

Her brown eyes scorned him. "Very well, I'll get it myself." She got up, starting for the bathroom.

McBride caught her and held her, quite firmly this time. "Be nice, sister. McGillicuddy's all right." His teeth shone whitely in what was meant to be a reassuring smile. "We don't want any trouble with the cops, do we?"

She dug her own teeth into McBride's wrist. "Let me go. Let me go, do you hear? You—you beast!"

McBride looked down at his wrist, discovering that the marks of her teeth showed quite plainly. "Well, for Christ's sake!" He took a deep breath. "Now see here, sister—"

"And don't you dare call me sister!"

McBride held her even more tightly. "I'll call you some very bad names indeed, baby, if you don't quit. This is for your own good, understand?"

Presently she relaxed panting against his chest. "All right, I'm sorry."

"That's better," McBride said. He still held her, though, and gradually it was borne in on him that he was holding her from choice, not from necessity. It was rather pleasant, even with the dead man there on the floor and with poor Mr. McGillicuddy coming anguished to life. In the elevator shaft outside, the rheumatic car clanked down, then up again. "That must be the cops," McBride said.

He put the girl regretfully from him as two uniformed men debouched from the elevator. Here and there along the hall, doors were beginning to open, and guests in various stages of undress were poking their heads out and demanding to know what went on. McBride waved a hand at the two cops. "In here."

They came over. They examined McBride carefully, then the girl, then Mr. McGillicuddy, who was now fully awake and moaning piteously. Finally they got around to the dead man. One of them sucked in his breath and looked at McBride with a new interest. "Fight over the dame, hunh? Who did it, you or the panty-waist?"

"Neither," McBride said, exercising great repression. "Offhand, I'd say the coroner's jury would blame party or parties unknown."

"Oh, you would, hunh? Whose room is this?"

"Mine."

The other copper said tiredly. "You better call in, Heinie. This is not for the likes of you and me." He turned and thrust out his jaw at the rapidly growing group of spectators. "Gwan, get back in your rooms. We'll be around and tell you all about it later."

Heinie was not through yet. He glared angrily at McBride. "You touch anything?"

"Yes," McBride said. "The doorknob, the light switch and the telephone." He smiled at the girl. "You see?"

She did not return the smile. Mr. McGillicuddy, in the presence of the Law, was rapidly becoming more man than mouse. He took off his glasses and began polishing them furiously. "See here, officer, I—"

"Shut up," Heinie said. He looked at McBride. "You act like you half knew your way around, bo. Where you from?"

"Los Angeles by way of Seattle," McBride said. "I got into Frisco—"

"San Francisco."

McBride remembered that San Franciscans did not like their city referred to as Frisco. "All right, I got into San Francisco about an hour ago. Apparently this is the only hotel within the city limits that isn't full up. I don't know why, although I'm beginning to have an idea. My name is McBride and I am thirty-two years old, single, no college education." His eyes were hard and bright and direct. "And I think your partner is smarter than you are. He knows his limitations."

Heinie reached for the sap in his hip pocket. "I got something here that's just made for smart guys."

McBride was frankly unimpressed. "That must be where you carry your brains too, copper. You're letting a homicide get cold while you throw your weight around."

The second cop nodded. "He's right, Heinie. Either you or me had better call in."

Heinie's shoulders lost some of their belligerence. "All right." He turned toward the elevator but paused to toss a parting shot at McBride. "I'll keep you in mind, bo." He and the elevator passed from sight.

McBride lit a cigarette and offered one to the remaining cop, who took it and put it in his cap. "You mustn't mind

Heinie," the cop said. "Some of us bulls get that way when we've been left in uniform too long. Heinie's been pounding a beat for twenty years."

"Forget it," McBride said magnanimously. He looked at the girl. "Why didn't I see you when I registered, sister?"

"I just came in a little while ago, myself," she said. "I'm the part-time bookkeeper." A smile tugged at the corners of her mouth and her eyes were frankly amused. "My name is Susan Lee, I am twenty-four years old, a graduate of Stanford and I work for a firm of public accountants. I live in San Francisco."

McBride admired her. "I think I'm going to like you, baby." He corrected himself, "Susan."

Somewhere—it sounded as though it might be on the floor above—a woman screamed.

The cop looked harried. Mr. McGillicuddy said, "Oh, my God!" again and rolled his eyes heavenward.

Susan Lee caught her breath. "I'll bet that's that Mrs. Foley in 517." Her brown eyes disapproved of Mr. McGillicuddy. "You really ought to do something about the Foleys."

The cop appealed to McBride. "Take a run upstairs, will you? It might be just a guy kicking his wife's teeth in. On the other hand it might have something to do with"—he waved a fist at the dead man inside McBride's room—"with this." He sighed. "If I leave here I'll catch hell. And if it turns out I should have left here and didn't I'll catch even more hell." His eyes glowed. "That goddam Heinie!"

The one elevator was still somewhere below. McBride went up the stairs two at a time, though the woman above had stopped after that one scream, so it was probable that whatever had caused it was now over and done with.

2

THERE WAS NOT an open door on the entire fifth floor. McBride began to wonder if he hadn't imagined the scream, but it didn't seem possible that four people could have imagined the same thing. In one of the rooms a party was going on and a radio blared Tommy Dorsey. In another there was the sound of low voices and the unmistakable riffle of cards being shuffled. McBride wished he had been thoughtful enough to make reservations at one of the better hotels. He envied the Cyrus H.Q. Chandlers. The Chandlers were at the St. Mark.

Coming back around an ell in the dimly-lit corridor he almost ran into the tallest, thinnest man he had ever seen. He had the distinct impression that this man had just come out of one of the rooms, perhaps because the man was standing with his back to a closed door. "You hear a woman scream up here?"

The tall man nodded gravely. He had a sort of funereal look about him, the air of an undertaker's assistant directing mourners to their seats. He pointed a lean forefinger. "In there."

The indicated door was numbered 517. McBride remembered that Susan Lee had said the Foleys, presumably husband and wife, were in 517. He rapped sharply. Turning to say something to the tall thin man he discov-

ered that the tall thin man was no longer there. He had
vanished as completely and as soundlessly as a shadow.
The door of 517 opened the merest crack. McBride put a
foot against it. "You the gal who's been doing the scream-
ing around here?"

She was a big woman, what McBride could see of her;
tall and blonde and heavy-breasted. Eyes as China-blue
as a doll's examined him casually. "Who wants to know,
dearie?"

"I'm the house dick," McBride said. He shoved a little
harder on the door and suddenly the woman let go of it
and he went sprawling into the room.

"The house dick!" the woman said. She laughed shrilly.
"This dump can't even afford an elevator boy—and he
claims he's the house dick!"

McBride, getting to his feet, saw that he and the woman
were not alone. There was a man on the bed; a very small,
very dapper man whose jet eyes were as hard and cynical
and unwinking as a pair of aces on ivory dice. He was fully
dressed except for his coat, which hung over the back of
a chair. An empty shoulder clip lay against the left side
of his vest and his right hand was buried under an open
newspaper. McBride didn't need three guesses to reach the
conclusion that the paper concealed something besides the
hand. He drew a slow breath and expelled it gently through
his nose. "Well!"

The small man propped himself more comfortably
against the pillows. "So you're the house dick."

McBride looked at the woman. There was a red mark
on her cheek, just below the left eye. It was quite apparent
that this was not a birthmark. "He hit you?"

Her gaudy kimono flapped open as she spread her hands. She would have made quite an armful. "I ran into a door." She pointed at the bathroom. "That one."

"But it was you that screamed?"

"Sure." She became coy all of a sudden and folded the kimono tightly about her. "Can't a lady scream in the privacy of her own room?"

The little man rustled the newspaper. "Shut up, Marge." His jet eyes bored into McBride. "Well?"

"You can put the rod away," McBride said. "There's been a kill downstairs and the cops thought the scream might mean another one. They sent me up."

Foley looked mildly interested. "You a dick?"

"Not local," McBride said. "I just happen to be living here the same as you." He made a bitter mouth. "The guy picked my room to get killed in." He half turned toward the door. "Guy named Severn from 514. Know him?" He could have sworn the woman gasped, but when he looked at her face it was as blank and vacuous as a department store dummy's. Her eyes were fixed on her husband—if he was her husband—with a sort of awed fascination.

The little man yawned. "Never heard of him, pal." He put the gun back in the shoulder clip, frankly bored by the whole thing, rolled over on one hip and began to peruse the newspaper anew. The woman opened the door. "Goodnight, dearie."

"And happy landings," McBride said. He backed out and the door closed in his face. Turning away he was confronted by still another door, the one before which the tall thin man had been standing. Perhaps it was because the thin man had obscured it that McBride hadn't noticed the number before. He noted it now. It was 514, the room directly above his own, the room belonging to the dead man, Severn. Lips moving in silent profanity he tried the knob but it refused to turn. He considered trying his own key in the lock; in fact he had already gotten the key out of his pocket when a whiskey voice said, almost in his ear, "Find what you were looking for, chum?"

McBride was undeniably startled, but he refused to admit it to anybody other than himself. "Another bogeyman?" He shivered. "Brrrr, am I scared!" Only then did he turn to face the newcomer, a squat, chunky man in baggy blue serge. The derby hat, pushed far back on his head, was reminiscent of yesterday's cop, and his inky-black hair clung to his scalp in tight, oily little ringlets. Fat brown cheeks pushed at his eyes, making them small and red, and fat lips worried a toothpick. "Tough guy, hunh?"

McBride denied this. "Just amazed," he said. Only an imp of Satan could have prompted his next remark. "First derby I've seen in ten years."

The fat man hit him then, smack in the mouth. As McBride fell back against the door he decided never again to judge a man by his exterior. This guy's appearance might be 1910, but there was nothing wrong with his technique. He hadn't telegraphed the blow by so much as a lifted eyebrow. McBride sucked at a cut lip. "Excuse it, Captain. My mistake."

"It's still your mistake," the fat man said. He rolled the toothpick deftly to the other side of his mouth. "The name is Orsatti and the rank is lieutenant." His small mahogany eyes practically stripped the clothes from McBride's back, looking for a gun. Then, satisfied that there wasn't one, he nodded his head at the closed door. "Open her up again."

McBride used a handkerchief on his mouth. "Not again," he said evenly. "When you arrived I was just about to try the first time."

"I won't argue with you," Orsatti said. "First or second, we can talk about that later. Unlock the door."

Shrugging, McBride put the key of 414 in the lock of 514. He was not too surprised when it worked perfectly. "They must have bought these locks from a mail-order catalogue."

"Sure," Orsatti said. "What did you expect in a drop like this?" He prodded McBride's kidneys. "Well, what are we waiting for?"

McBride pushed the door inward. Inside, the lights were full on, and a fog-laden breeze from the bay whipped the sleazy curtains at an open window. Someone had been even more careless with the dead man's effects than he had with McBride's. The room was quite a mess.

Orsatti's voice was not unpleasant. It had a peculiar husky quality, as though alcohol had done to his tonsils what the scientists claim it does to your brain, but it didn't rasp the ears. It was what Orsatti said that counted. "So you weren't in here before?"

"No."

"You're a liar," Orsatti said calmly. He took out his gun. "Let's go downstairs, chum. I want you to meet the corpse."

A chill that had nothing to do with the fog-laden breeze ran icy little fingers up and down McBride's spine. He licked his lips. "Meaning you think I did it?"

Orsatti rolled his toothpick. "Meaning you're the likeliest prospect we've got so far. Though I still don't know why you used a knife," he added. "There's two guns in your grip."

McBride could recognize a spot as well as the next man. He did something then that he never did except in the greatest extremity. He admitted his profession to a stranger, his voice sounding a little feverish, even to his own ears. "Now look, I can explain that. I'm a private operative. I've got a license for those rods."

Orsatti was unimpressed. "Maybe that's why you didn't use them," he said. He lifted his gun a trifle. "Let's go down, chum."

They went down.

The deputy medical examiner was a smallish, gray-haired man with pince-nez and a peppery disposition. "I say this man was drunk!" he informed Orsatti. He meant the corpse, Mr. Severn. He had the knife they had taken out of Mr. Severn's back and he waved this to emphasize his point. It was an enormous clasp knife with a bone handle and a blade at least six inches long.

"All right," Lieutenant Orsatti said in his husky voice, "he was drunk. I'll even go you one better and admit that he was dead drunk. At least he is now." He looked around the crowded room as though expecting everybody to roar with mirth at this sally. No one did.

A red-haired man in a captain's uniform was listening to Heinie and the other harness bull making their report, and there were the usual print men, photographers and what not. McBride chose a chair over by the windows and sulked. He was rapidly becoming fed up with all this horseplay over a dead man he didn't even know. He saw that what the unknown vandal hadn't accomplished in the way of wrecking the room had been taken care of by the Headquarters detail.

Mr. McGillicuddy was nowhere in sight, but Susan Lee was still there. Presently she came over and stood beside McBride, not looking at him in particular, just standing there. "Did you see the Foleys?"

McBride admitted sourly that he had seen them.

"What did you think of them?"

"She's a tramp. He's a gunsel and a hop-head."

Susan sighed. "This is not a very good hotel."

"You're telling me!" After a while he demanded indignantly, "You think I'd be here if I could have gotten anything else?" He looked at her. "You know what I think? I think the guy that invented conventions should have been taken out and drowned when he was very small—like kittens."

Lieutenant Orsatti overheard this. "So you don't like our conventions, either."

McBride got to his feet. His eyes had a curiously muddy look and he was angrier than he had been in months. "Listen, you bastard! I had the misfortune to be born in Los Angeles, but I'm getting tired of paying for it every time I land in this lousy town of yours. Even your cab drivers take it as a personal affront if I inadvertently say Frisco instead of San Francisco. You are so smug you still think this is the only city on the Pacific Coast, and you're too dumb to look in the census books and find out different." He took a breath. "And now, since you ask me, I will tell you the God's truth about your conventions, your bridges and your town. I don't like them."

Somebody clapped hands and McBride saw that it was the deputy medical examiner. He thought that probably he

had made a fool of himself but he was so furious over being
delayed in the conduct of his own affairs that he didn't care.
He strode over to the red-haired man in uniform. "Maybe
I'm wrong about this. Maybe we should all stand around
and discuss the weather. You see, I come from a place where
they think murder is a damned sight more important than
a juvenile pride in the burg where it happened."

"We heard you," the captain said. He lifted a hairy hand
to quiet the murmur of voices around them but he did not
take his eyes from McBride's face. "We're still listening,
Mr. McBride."

McBride said carefully, "I got into town something over
an hour ago. After trying the St. Mark, the St. Francis and
all the other hotels within the radius of a mile I finally
found a hacker who told me about this place. I registered
and came up and left my bag. I then went out and bought
a drink. When I came back I found the dead guy in my
room. I called the cops." His smile did not quite reach his
eyes. "And that, so help me Christ, is all I know about—"
He broke off as he remembered the very tall, very thin man
he had met in the corridor upstairs. "No, it isn't. There was
a long skinny drink of water in the hall outside 514 when
I went up." He described the thin man.

Orsatti's toothpick snapped. "Shaped something like a
herring, wasn't he? A red herring?" He had been talking
to Susan Lee and he now leered at her in a particularly
unpleasant manner. "You happen to know if there's a guy
like that registered here?"

She said she didn't know. Orsatti snapped his fingers at
one of the harness bulls. "Get the manager up here again."
And when Mr. McGillicuddy appeared, still wearing his

pale and frightened and ineffectual look, Orsatti put the question to him. Mr. McGillicuddy said that there was no such guest registered. He said he had never seen such a man hanging about. They let him go. "All right," Orsatti said, "now we'll talk to the Foleys." But when the harness bull returned this time he was empty-handed. The Foleys, it seemed, had flown.

Lieutenant Orsatti came in for a few bad moments then. The red-haired captain, whose name turned out to be Wick, gave him hell for concentrating on McBride while everybody else in the place had either slipped out or had the chance to slip out. Orsatti took it standing up, but in front of a dozen people, including two or three reporters, he wasn't liking it very well.

Not looking at McBride, but very conscious of him, he said, "All right, but I still think we've got the key to the whole business right here under our noses." Angry color mottled his fat olive cheeks and his husky voice had a choked sound. "The Foleys ran out on purpose-not just to get away, but to take the heat off this guy." He enlarged on this theory. "Same like the dame screamed in the first place. That was to give McBride his chance to get clear of Heinie and the other bull."

Something about that caught and held Wick's attention. He stared very hard at McBride. "I just talked to the chief of dicks down in L.A. He says you're a pretty slippery customer."

"He would," McBride said. He was surprised that Gahagan hadn't told them to toss him in the can and throw the key away. Gahagan didn't like McBride very well. He said, being carefully polite, "Orsatti hasn't explained why I found it necessary to slash my own bag and call the cops."

"Well, no, but— By the way, just what is your business in San Francisco, Mr. McBride?"

"My own," McBride said. His mouth drooped. "You ought to know better than ask a question like that, Skipper." He spread the fingers of his left hand and began folding them back one by one as he enumerated. "I did call the cops. I did see the man I described in the upper hall. I was not, as the lieutenant claims, coming out of Severn's room; I was about to enter it. And as for Severn's being in *my* room, your own medical examiner explains that. Severn was drunk. He got in the automatic elevator and punched the wrong button by mistake."

The telephone rang. Captain Wick went to it and identified himself. "Oh, it's you again, Gahagan." He listened a moment, furrows of disapproval creasing his brow. "Well, if you ask me, this is a hell of a time for a rib like that. Well, if you say so, sure, but—" He put his sand-colored eyes on McBride. "Gahagan says you're okay; says he was just ribbing you—and me." He extended the receiver. "He wants to talk to you."

McBride accepted the instrument gingerly, for this whitewashing was nothing like the Los Angeles chief of dicks he knew. "Hello?"

The answering voice was no more Gahagan's than it was the Queen of Sheba's. It was a sly voice, and smug and full of false joviality. It belonged to Mr. Erin Rourke, a vice president of the Underwriters' Alliance. "Well, Rex!"

McBride was uncomfortably aware of a dozen pairs of eyes on the back of his neck, and of the probability that there was a cop listening in on the switchboard downstairs. He moistened his lips. "How are you, Chief? I was just telling this roomful of people that—"

"All right, all right," Rourke said, "I can take a hint." His voice became confidential. "How you making out with the Chandlers?"

"Not so good," McBride said.

"Of course not," Rourke said cheerfully. "I told you all along you were off on the wrong foot. The Chandlers aren't the kind of people that would steal their own jewelry just for the insurance."

Had McBride been alone he could have told Rourke some interesting facts about the Chandler family; facts he had picked up in Seattle, and in Los Angeles, before following them to Seattle. He was obliged to admit, however, that none of them seemed to have any bearing on their loss of the Adelphi necklace. He said, "Well, thanks for squaring me, Chief," and was about to hang up when Rourke yelled at him.

"Who was this guy you killed?"

McBride yelled right back. "I didn't!" It occurred to him that the cop downstairs, if there was one, must be getting quite an earful. "By the way, how did you—?"

"Oh, that," Rourke said carelessly. He giggled. "Why, somebody up there called Gahagan, and Gahagan called me, to give me the horselaugh, and so with my customary aplomb I became Gahagan and telephoned your captors." His voice became tinged with suspicion. "You're sure this hasn't anything to do with—"

"Positive," McBride said.

Rourke sighed. "I thought it might be Slugs Foley."

McBride licked suddenly parched lips. "Who?"

"Foley," Rourke said impatiently. "The cops had a tip from a stoolie that Slugs might have been implicated, but they can't seem to find him."

3

"IT MUST BE interesting," Susan said, "being a private detective."

"Oh, it is," McBride assured her.

They were at a table in the Stardust Room atop the Hotel St. Mark, and beneath them, beyond the tall chromium and plate-glass window, the city fell away in undulant waves of bright neon and the diamond glitter of a million street lights. An incoming fog shrouded the upper reaches of the Bay Bridge and the Golden Gate, but up here on the hill it was still crystal clear. On the dance floor perhaps thirty or forty couples moved leisurely to the strains of Harry Owens' *Sweet Leilani,* and McBride, always a sucker for melody rather than straight rhythm, was affected to the point where he covered Susan's hand with one of his own.

"You're very beautiful, you know," he said gently. As a matter of fact, she was. Without the pencil in her hair, and the black sateen sleevelets, and against the background of a Labrador mink coat which looked a trifle expensive for a bookkeeper, she was easily the loveliest lady in the room. Besides, McBride needed her in his business.

She did not remove her hand, but her next words destroyed some of the romance of the moment. "You really are callous, aren't you?"

McBride slumped in the chair, battered and bruised. They had been working on him for half an hour while O'Hara watched.

McBride was indignant. "Because I'm not weeping over your poor Mr. Severn?"

She shook her head. "He isn't my poor Mr. Severn. As far as I'm concerned the company could cross the whole Trojan Hotel off its list."

McBride pointed an accusing finger at her. "Now who's being callous?"

"Except Mr. McGillicuddy," Susan said. "I always rather liked Mr. McGillicuddy."

At a table some little distance away a maitre was seating two ladies and a gentleman. McBride pretended to be very

interested in his companion, but he was quite conscious of the new arrivals. He did not know the gentleman, but the ladies were Delilah and Celeste Chandler, and in spite of Erin Rourke and the Slugs Foley incident, McBride would have given you six, two and even that it was one of these ladies who had arranged the loss of the Adelphi necklace. He had nothing to prove this. It was merely his belief that no professional would be fool enough to steal it. The Adelphi was one of the better-known collector's items.

Delilah Chandler was a woman of thirty-five, taller than average and quite striking looking in a Philadelphia-stock,

Camel-ad sort of way. Instinctively you knew that she
played golf and polo and devoted her spare time to relief
of the underprivileged. She looked as though she would
know all about sex, too, though she would probably want
to be intellectual about it. She had a crown of very dark
hair, gray-green eyes and a mouth that had a tendency to
be arrogant. Across the tables and the shoulders of intervening guests her gray-green eyes met McBride's darker
ones fleetingly and without apparent sign of recognition.

The younger woman, Celeste, was something else
again. She would not want to be intellectual about sex,
ever. The way she moved her body, the way her sloe-black
eyes roved the room, showed that she was conscious of it
every moment. She had the lithe quick grace of a panther.
McBride's neck still bore the marks of her claws, result of
having mentioned in her hearing that the Chandler theft
looked to him like an inside job. Celeste was an adopted
daughter. Three or four years back it had been fashionable
to adopt Belgians, or Hollanders, or almost anybody except
undernourished Americans. Celeste was Belge.

Susan Lee said in a small-girl voice, "Who are they,
please?"

On the point of putting a piece of very rare steak into his
mouth, McBride paused and regarded her with a certain
respect. "Who are whom?"

"Don't quibble," Susan said. "I saw you looking at them."
She kneaded a piece of French roll into a ball. "And I saw
them looking at you."

"Oh, them," McBride said. He shrugged. "Some people
I met down in Los Angeles. Husband's a WPB coordinator or something."

"Is that the husband?" Her brown eyes had golden flecks in them now. She was laughing at him. "And if so, just whose husband is he?"

"No," McBride said, denying that the man was the husband of either. "I don't know who he is, but he seems typical of their usual crowd. A little on the South American side, wouldn't you say?"

Susan nodded emphatically. "Cesar Romero."

"Probably somebody important," McBride said. "That's the only kind WPB officials know." He had the waiter bring ices and it was some little time before he said with a fine affectation of carelessness, "How do you feel about people with two middle initials?"

"Pure swank," Susan said.

"My sentiments exactly," McBride said. He waxed enthusiastic. "By God, the more I see of you, baby, the more I realize how much we have in common." He pushed the thought from him that it was really the two middle initials of Cyrus H.Q. Chandler which were motivating him in this case. By and large he considered nearly all Washington appointees a bunch of alphabetic fumblers, but to have one with two middle initials thrust down his throat was nothing short of a personal affront. His smile was faintly reminiscent of a wolf's. "Yes, sir, we've got a lot in common!"

Involuntarily Susan shivered. "We have, haven't we? Poor Mr. Severn, for instance."

"I wish you wouldn't keep bringing him up," McBride said. "You've practically ruined my appetite."

"I noticed."

"Well, you have." And then, because he had been very good and only had two cocktails to stimulate an appetite which Susan—and Lieutenant Orsatti and the dead man and Erin Rourke—had ruined, he ordered brandy with their coffee. "About the Foleys," he said presently, watching her while seeming to be very interested in the light refractions in his brandy glass. "What made you think it was she who screamed?"

"I'd heard her scream before. They were always fighting."

"They'd been there long?"

"Well, no;" Susan said, "less than a week this time." But they had stayed at the Trojan before. They were what might be termed recurrent guests, and it was Susan's impression that whenever they were in San Francisco or its vicinity they made the Hotel Trojan their headquarters.

"They seem to have any connection with this Mr. Severn?"

Susan couldn't say, not from her personal knowledge. She thought, however, that if there had been a connection Mr. McGillicuddy would have mentioned it to the police. Susan's face gave no indication that there was anything strange in McBride's sudden renewal of interest in the murder. "Was that really the Los Angeles police department who called back?"

McBride hurriedly drained his glass. "Certainly." Inwardly he cursed Erin Rourke for having taken the chance. There was no reason to suppose that Captain Wick, or Lieutenant Orsatti or somebody wouldn't be as smart as this girl across the table from him. The call could easily be checked back and of course the Los Angeles department would deny it. Come to think of it, Orsatti had been entirely too complacent in agreeing to McBride's release. All he had been asked was to stay in town for the inquest.

"Because," Susan said, as though continuing a train of thought, "it was your bag that was slashed; it was your room that Mr. Severn was killed in." She studied McBride's face from beneath demurely lowered lashes. "What do you suppose they were looking for?"

McBride himself had been pondering this problem. Certain aspects of it lent credibility to Rourke's tip that Slugs Foley had been implicated in the theft of the Adelphi necklace. On the other hand, it seemed to be stretching coincidence a little too far to find the thieves and a possible hijacker and Rex McBride, all interested in the same thing, domiciled through sheer accident in the same third-rate hotel. True, the Foleys apparently had made the Trojan their headquarters from time to time. Also, the current overcrowded condition of the city's better hotels had made necessary McBride's choice of a flop-house whose only bid for favor was that it did not lie on the wrong side of Market Street—"South of the Slot," as the natives put it.

McBride's own experience, indeed tonight's alone, would convince anybody that there was nothing whatever to this social distinction. He said, "I haven't the faintest idea what they were looking for, precious!" This being the truth he felt virtuous as hell. He felt that virtue should not go unrewarded. He ordered another brandy.

Around and about them swirled the noise of an ultra-fashionable restaurant at the fashionably late dinner hour. It was well after nine o'clock. The susurrant sound of dancing feet was like the swish of surf on a sandy beach, a fitting background for the orchestra's *Song of the Islands*. Muted laughter and the tinkle of glassware lent a carnival air to the occasion. McBride's eyes were somber as he noted that the Stardust Room was filling up with a preponderance of ladies whose escorts were officers in uniform. He himself was still waiting to hear from Washington. It was beginning to look as though he would be waiting when the war was over.

Susan leaned her elbows on the table, her chin on interlocked fingers. "Tell me about being a private detective."

"It's a dog's life," McBride said. He was inclined to be morose about the whole thing. "You're a cross between a social pariah and a thief, and nobody who is anybody will have anything to do with you—until they're in a jam for doing exactly the kind of things they sneer at you for doing in order to get them out." He glowered at Celeste Chandler, who was dancing with the guy who ought to be Cesar Romero, but wasn't. Delilah Chandler, left at the table alone, was watching the couple, too. The expression on her face was not pleasant.

It was obvious that Susan Lee didn't believe a word McBride had said. "Even Captain Wick didn't press you to disclose the reason for your being in San Francisco."

"You ought to see the way Orsatti pressed me." McBride's lower lip was still slightly swollen. "And don't let that guy Wick fool you, either. There are some that are harder to get along with than others, but there isn't a cop in the world who really likes the private boys." He sighed heavily into his inhaler. "It just isn't in the cards."

"Why?"

McBride looked at her. "For one thing, the good ones make more money than they do. For another, our interests are sometimes—most of the time—opposed." He was watching her face carefully now, though his eyes seemed intent on the little hollow at the base of her throat. "Take me, for instance. I work for insurance companies mostly. Naturally the object is to save the underwriters money—to recover in toto, if you can, but at least to minimize the loss."

"And the police?"

"Are interested in getting the thief, or the embezzler or whatever. Sometimes they do, but more often they don't. And even if they do, it doesn't necessarily follow that the thief and the fruits of his thievery are still keeping company."

Her eyes were bright with excitement. "It's kind of a game, isn't it?"

"Sure," McBride said. At the moment he thought it a pretty shabby game. He decided that his ego needed a little inflation. He began telling her about a chase he had made across the Pacific after a man who had stolen two million dollars. He remembered that most of the two hundred thousand he had made out of that job was now gone, and this brought him to the manner in which he had lost a large part of it, the gambling syndicate headed by Sean O'Hara. He was describing O'Hara, with gestures, when O'Hara himself got out of the express elevator. This certainly seemed to be the night for coincidences.

Susan said, "What's the matter?"

I must be losing my grip, McBride thought. This gal can read my face like a first-grade primer. Aloud he said, "The guy I was just telling you about is making a personal appearance. You can see for yourself." But the real reason his mask had momentarily slipped was not O'Hara's presence in San Francisco. The big man had some clubs up here too, so that part of it was perfectly natural. The thing that startled McBride was Sean O'Hara's effect on Celeste Chandler. She had been dancing smoothly, graceful and sure-footed as a lynx, and suddenly she became very clumsy indeed, clinging to her partner and almost tripping him. Her partner's back was toward O'Hara, and to McBride it seemed that her object was to keep it that way. For just a moment her face was convulsed with what looked like mingled terror and rage; then she buried it against Tall-Dark-and-Handsome's chest and succeeded in practically pushing him from the floor. The crowd swallowed them.

O'Hara himself had not even nodded, though there was little or no doubt in McBride's mind that the big man was fully aware of the incident. From experience he knew that O'Hara could be aware of a lot of things without its showing on his face.

Susan's voice reminded McBride that she was still there. "He looks like a top."

McBride smiled at her. "He does, doesn't he?"

They watched O'Hara being escorted to a small table in the corner of the tall glass-and-chromium windows overlooking the bay. The maitre was a slight, nervously gesticulate man and the effect was somewhat that of a furiously puffing tug nosing an ocean liner into its berth. Not that O'Hara was clumsy; he was just sort of indomitable, like Gibraltar. Above a broad expanse of starched white shirt front his face was a granite cliff with the sun on it; thinning, smoothly brushed white hair carried the illusion still further; a sifting of powder snow under the sun. And though, as Susan had said, he was built like a top, he did

not teeter as so many fat men do who have unconsciona-
bly small feet. He sat, and for just a moment his eyes met
McBride's directly. He nodded. McBride nodded. Then
each appeared to forget the other entirely.

Susan shivered. "I don't believe I should like to have that
man hate me."

"No," McBride said. He wondered if O'Hara hated
Celeste Chandler. He wondered who the tall, dark and
handsome gentleman was; the one with whom Celeste
had disappeared. He bethought himself to look at Delilah
Chandler and found that she, too, knew Sean O'Hara,
though she was doing her best to conceal the fact. She had
been joined by her husband.

Cyrus H.Q. Chandler had what might be termed the
senatorial look. McBride's information placed the man as
having once been Southern California's leading automobile distributor, but probably due to Delilah's influence he
had left the marts of trade for various appointments in
the diplomatic service. Since there were few countries left
where such a man could function, and since the administration declined to fire anybody, he was now an official
in the WPB. It was rumored that his automobile distrib-
utorship, of which he still retained a controlling interest,
was gradually eating up his surplus. There weren't any more
automobiles to be distributed, but Old Man Overhead was
still as hungry as ever. McBride thought that maybe this
was one of the reasons the Adelphi necklace had disappeared. A hundred thousand dollars' insurance wasn't hay,
even with inflation.

Susan said, a trifle wistfully, "Could we have just one
teeny-weeny little dance before curfew rings?"

"Sure," McBride said. He rose and folded her into his arms and they began to dance. The perfume of her hair reminded him a little of Kay Ford's, though the hair was not the same color. He decided he would not think of Kay Ford, except that he was angry with her for refusing to accompany him on this trip. He said, mocking Susan's interest in his profession, "Tell me about being an accountant, beautiful."

"It's a dog's life," Susan said, repeating his own observation. "Murders and men who look like brooding Sioux keep getting between you and the figures." She neither obtruded her rather lovely body on his consciousness, nor withheld it. She said, "So you're looking for something that has been stolen."

"Maybe," McBride said cautiously.

"And somebody thought you had found it," Susan said.

Until this moment the possibility had not occurred to McBride. He was a trifle startled. The hand at the small of her back pressed her a little closer to him. "What makes you think that, hon?"

"Your slashed bag."

He shook his head. "That was supposed to be Severn's, not mine." He wondered if it had been the Foleys or the very tall, very thin shadow in the Trojan's upper hall who had stuck the knife into Severn's back. He remembered the open window in Severn's room and it occurred to him that Mr. Severn might have been killed there and later carried down to his room because Severn's had been too close to that of the Foleys. He wondered if he didn't owe the Foleys a little something for that. He decided to let the police handle it.

As for Erin Rourke's theory, it was diametrically opposed to Susan's, for if Slugs Foley had stolen the Adelphi necklace he would know damned well that McBride hadn't recovered it.

The music stopped, leaving Susan and McBride and half a dozen other couples stranded within arm's reach of the Chandlers' table. Cyrus H.Q. Chandler recognized McBride and he half rose, an angry flush mottling his square senatorial face. "Young man, are you following me?"

McBride was, and he had made no effort to conceal the fact, but he pretended to be greatly astonished. "Should I be?"

"I saw you in Seattle!"

"I saw you, too," McBride said. With his arm still about Susan's waist he smiled down at Delilah. "Mrs. Chandler, Mr. Chandler—Miss Lee." All three acknowledged the introduction with less than half their minds.

Chandler was furious. "I won't have it. Your assumption that any of my family or friends had anything to do with the theft is not only ridiculous, it's insulting." The muscles along his jaw line bulged lumpily. "I shall take steps to put a stop to this surveillance."

McBride's face was slightly malicious. "What kind of steps?"

"There are ways," Chandler said darkly. He sat down unwillingly as Delilah, acutely conscious that they were the cynosure of a dozen pairs of eyes, tugged at his sleeve.

McBride said, "Well, it's been nice seeing you again," and led Susan back to his table. Paying his check he was accosted by an assistant manager of the St. Mark, who announced that there had just been a cancellation and if

Mr. McBride could handle a suite there was now one available. "Could I handle it!" McBride said enthusiastically. Watching Susan's face he was impelled to ask if there were any dead bodies cluttering up the place. "The flop-house I'm in now is littered with them."

The man thought he was kidding. "Really?"

"Honest to God," McBride said. He introduced Susan. "Ask her if you don't believe me." And then, for no reason at all, he said, "Who was silly enough to give up a comfortable bed on a night like this?"

"A Mr. O'Hara," the man said. "A Mr. Sean O'Hara."

McBride's eyes swept the far corner of the room. The gross figure of Sean O'Hara was no longer there.

4

IF MCBRIDE HAD issued invitations to a soiree he could scarcely have had more guests than he had between the hours of eleven and one. Having left instructions with the porter's desk regarding his bag at the Hotel Trojan, and two others at the railroad station, he had delivered Susan to her apartment high up the California Street hill and returned to the St. Mark via the same cab. In Susan's alert mind he had planted a seed of suspicion and intrigue which he hoped would bear fruit. He had no qualms about using her as an ally, conscious or otherwise, for unless she began improvising she would be in no danger. He simply felt that Susan, through her acquaintanceship with Mr. McGillicuddy, would be able to elicit more information about the Trojan's varied assortment of guests than he could himself, and though he was still somewhat skeptical of coincidence he decided that the best thing to do, if you couldn't explain coincidence, was to accept it. Besides, one man could only do so much, and he felt that he should continue to devote his attentions to the Chandler family. There were signs that his almost constant surveillance was wearing them down to the breaking point.

Unpacking his bags and sorting out those items which would require the skill of Valet Service, he occasionally paused to refresh himself from a tall beaded glass delivered a short time before by a bellhop whose name was Charley. The two guns which Lieutenant Nick Orsatti had deplored lay on the white uncut-mohair davenport under the sitting-room's windows. It was a nice suite. It reminded McBride of his position in life, a far cry from when he used to peddle papers and help roll drunks in the gutters of Los Angeles. He regretted the drunks. He was very grateful to Sean O'Hara for having relinquished the suite. He was thinking about O'Hara when there was a knock on the door. The knocker turned out to be none other than Sean O'Hara himself.

The fat man now wore a topcoat and white muffler and top hat, all but the hat making him more enormous and impressive than ever. His eyes had the color and warmth of steel bearings. "Talk to you a minute, McBride?"

"Sure," McBride said. His eyes took in the two men loitering at either end of the short corridor. "Want to ask your army in, too?"

"No."

McBride shrugged. He was in shirt-sleeves and this accentuated the darkness of his skin. He hoped his face was as impassive as O'Hara's. "Suit yourself." He closed the door behind O'Hara's bulk, pushed forward the strongest and most capacious chair in the room and offered to ring for a drink.

O'Hara accepted the chair but declined the drink. His large, very white hands rested squarely on his large plump knees. His inordinately small feet rested primly, neatly on the rose-taupe carpet. He did not remove the topper, so it was obvious that he did not expect to stay long. "I'm not trying to pry into your business, McBride, but if you're not working I've got a proposition for you."

McBride jerked a thumb at the hall door. "Something the boys out there can't handle?"

O'Hara looked at the two guns on the davenport. "My boys can shoot as well as you. They don't think as well."

"Coming from you," McBride said, "I'll accept that as a compliment." He sipped at his Collins. "I'm listening, Sean."

"Then you're not working?"

"Nothing that couldn't be postponed," McBride said carelessly. He grinned. "In spite of the dough you've taken me for in the last couple months, I owe you a favor." He waved at the opulence of the suite. "I was due to sleep in a flophouse that's probably full of fleas."

"I was thinking about the dough," O'Hara said. "Thinking about a way you could maybe get some of it back." The skin at the corners of his eyes crinkled a little and it seemed to McBride that the eyes themselves were a trifle less steely. "You're a good gambler, Rex. You don't yell when you're hurt. How'd you like to get in on the winning side for a change—come in with me?"

McBride was genuinely surprised. "Why?"

"The syndicate is washed up in Los Angeles," O'Hara said. "We've tried, but we can't buck the new administration any longer. We can't buy it." He looked at the door a little blankly, as though surprised that there was anything in the world that money couldn't buy. "A week or so ago our place out in the valley was knocked over by some heist artists. There was some shooting. That brought the cops in and the cops—the D.A.—offered us the choice of moving out or getting thrown out."

"So that was your place," McBride said. The Seattle papers had been careful not to mention names.

O'Hara went on as though there had been no interruption. "It's only a question of time before we have trouble up here, too." For the first time in minutes he looked at McBride directly. "So we're thinking about Nevada again."

"You tried that once," McBride said. He recalled the syndicate retiring licking its wounds, for while gambling was legalized in Nevada the local forces were well entrenched, politically and otherwise, and they hadn't taken kindly to outside competition.

"Yes," O'Hara admitted. After a while he said, "But things are different now. Magnesium and other war industries have brought a whole new vote into the state. If we can get hold of that we can lick the situation."

"So you want me to go to Reno."

"And Vegas, and Carson City." O'Hara took off his topper and with a large white hand smoothed the already smooth white hair that lay so close to his pink scalp. His voice was pleasant. "No rough stuff, you understand. Just a little preliminary investigation that will have no connection with the syndicate." He rose to his feet with amazing ease for one of such great bulk. "If we put it over it ought to work out pretty well for you."

"I'll think about it," McBride said.

With his hand on the doorknob O'Hara paused. "What does that mean? We're in something of a hurry, McBride. Elections don't wait."

McBride put his glass down carefully. "It means I'll

think about it, Sean." He really intended to; in fact he was already thinking about it when it occurred to him that Sean O'Hara's connections in and about San Francisco might include a knowledge of a certain Slugs Foley. "A guy was killed in this flophouse I was telling you about. Happened in my room. It's a toss-up with the police whether I did it or a hood named Slugs Foley. You wouldn't know any of his hangouts, would you?"

O'Hara appeared to consider the name. "No," he said presently, "no, I don't believe I know him." He twisted the doorknob back and forth a time or two. "Is that why you can't give me your answer right away?"

It seemed to McBride that the big man was a little too pressing; a little too intent on getting him out of town, but he could find no reason for it. Unless, of course, Celeste Chandler had told O'Hara that McBride was bothering her. Still, his observation of their sudden meeting in the Stardust Room upstairs hadn't indicated that they were exactly friends. He said, "The cops have warned me not to leave—at least until after the inquest. I thought that maybe if I could get hold of this guy Foley I could hurry it up a little for you."

O'Hara nodded. "I'll let you know if I hear of anything," he said. From a pin-seal wallet he extracted a card and held it out to McBride. "I've got a place down the Peninsula a ways. This will get you in." He went out.

McBride's next caller was a champion of ladies. He introduced himself by presenting a card which said he was Mr. Rodriguez Franz Sebastian, attached to the San Francisco consulate of Para. McBride had a little difficulty placing a country named Para. He thought maybe it was somewhere near Patagonia. He had no difficulty at all placing Rodriguez Franz Sebastian. He was the gentleman of the Stardust Room whom Susan had likened to Cesar Romero. He looked a little older, close up, and he had impeccable clothes and teeth, and a nice powerful pair of shoulders. His manner was more direct than that of most Latin-Americans. He said, "Mr. McBride, I must ask you to cease annoying the Chandlers."

McBride made no attempt to deny that he had been annoying the Chandlers. He said, "Why?"

"For your own good," Sebastian said promptly. His English was as impeccable as his teeth. "Mr. Chandler is a busy man—an important man—and rather than annoy him the ladies have appealed to me."

"Both of them?"

"Yes."

McBride smiled engagingly. "Confidentially, which one do you like best?" He watched Sebastian's eyes narrow slightly, and the tensing of muscles along the man's upper arms and shoulders. "I mean, which one would you rather I pinned the job on?"

It appeared that Mr. Sebastian had superb self-control, too. He scarcely raised his voice. "There are things that can happen to a man like you, Mr. McBride." Above his rather full mouth his mustache described a kind of Satanic V. "Not nice things." He shrugged. "This is not a threat, understand, but these are perilous times. I suggest that you and your assistants withdraw and turn your attentions else-where. The Chandlers did not steal their own necklace."

There was something very curious here—the part about McBride's assistants. He had no assistants. He wondered if the Los Angeles police might be working the same angle as himself, but he could not recall seeing anybody watching the Chandler entourage who even smelled like a copper. He sighed. "I'm beginning to believe you are right, pal."

Sebastian's smile gained warmth. "Now you are being intelligent." He felt called upon to explain that even innocent people dislike to be spied on. "I may say to the ladies, then, that you and the—others are leaving San Francisco?"

McBride said with great dignity and utter falsity, "You may say to them that they have ceased to interest me except as owners of the Adelphi necklace. My clients have paid off the loss, but naturally we are still trying to recover the jewels. If we do recover we shall expect a settlement from the Chandlers. Otherwise they have nothing to fear." Again he sighed. "As for leaving San Francisco, I only wish I could, but another matter has come up that—" He was faintly apologetic. "The police insist that I stick around."

"The police?"

"A guy got murdered," McBride said. "The police always get snotty about murders. It seems to bother them."

Mr. Sebastian agreed that this was understandable. He seemed relieved rather than otherwise that it was only a murder which was keeping McBride in town. He departed, his straight broad back reminding McBride faintly of a general with a sword. McBride decided that sometime he must look up the history and geography—especially the geography—of Para.

The champion of ladies hadn't been gone more than ten minutes when one of the ladies herself appeared. McBride let her in with some surprise and a mildly lecherous hope that something interesting would come of this, for Delilah Chandler was new to his experience of ladies who pay nocturnal visits to men in their rooms. She was in a gold-brocaded gown that was something less formal than the one she had been wearing in the Stardust Room. Her crown of dark hair, her gray-green eyes and faintly arrogant mouth were the same. She was considerably younger than her husband, possibly thirty-five. McBride saw nothing wrong with thirty-five as an age, especially such an abundantly blessed thirty-five as Delilah's. It occurred to him, oddly, that Cyrus H.Q. Chandler needed a haircut. He wondered if the Biblical Samson had had two middle initials.

Delilah took some little time before stating her mission. Her long-legged stride carried her about the suite, to the uncut-mohair divan on which McBride's two guns still lay, to the windows, very casually to the open bedroom door. She said, "Has Roddy been here?"

McBride lit a cigarette. "Roddy?"

"Sebastian," she said sharply.

"Oh, him!" McBride sat on the divan and leaned back, watching her with appreciative eyes. "Yes, Roddy was here."

"What did he want?"

McBride was surprised. "Why, didn't you know? I thought you sent him." He attempted to blow a smoke ring but was unsuccessful. "You and Celeste."

Delilah's rather fine breasts rose and fell in a little sigh. "Celeste is such a trial," she said. "So willful, so impetuous." Gray-green eyes considered McBride with considerably more friendliness that they had heretofore shown. "Believe me, I am sorry she scratched you, Mr. McBride. I feel that in a measure that is what has motivated you to—to hound us, rather than any innate belief that she—that we might be criminally implicated."

McBride said nothing to this. As a matter of fact, there was a modicum of truth in the accusation.

Delilah said, continuing the subject of Celeste, "It was my husband's idea that we adopt her, you know."

So you don't like her, McBride thought. That was all right with him, Delilah's not liking her adopted daughter; he didn't like her either. He just wondered why Delilah was taking the trouble to tell him so now.

"Though she was really very sweet when she was younger," Delilah said. "She came to us after Dunkirk. Recommended by some very dear friends we had known on the Continent."

McBride's smile was a trifle wolfish. "Her people wouldn't happen to have been in the diamond trade, would they?"

Delilah was hurt. "That is hardly fair of you, Mr. McBride. You make it seem as though—as if—"

"You're practically telling me she did it," McBride said brutally. "What I want to know is why?"

Delilah began to shake, suddenly and uncontrollably, as a tree shakes in a furious gust of wind. "Because the little bitch is trying to seduce my husband!"

"And Roddy too, perhaps?" He got up and put an arm around her, finding it very pleasant, as always, to hold a sobbing—sobbing *and* beautiful woman to his breast. A strand of her lovely hair clung damply to his nose, tickling it. His eyes were bright and hard and calculating. "Jealousy is worse than liquor," he said. "It biteth like an adder."

She leaned against him a little harder. "I am not jealous."

Presently, as though growing a bit too conscious of him, she pushed him away and demanded a handkerchief. "I don't know what you must think of me. I—"

"What I think of you either way isn't important," McBride said. His eyes caressed her shapeliness. His voice was matter-of-fact. "If you can show me any proof I'll help you sink her. But I won't stick my neck out just to help you get rid of a little competition. That's flat."

The handkerchief had left little smudges of mascara beneath her eyes. They were not unattractive. She was still a lady in distress, but a very well-bred lady, one who could not possibly have sullied her lips with such a naughty word as bitch. "I'm sorry; I haven't any proof, of course. I was just a little—well, a little upset."

"Yes," McBride said.

She moved slowly toward the door, possibly expecting him to make some effort to detain her, but when he did not she said, "Good-night," in a restrained sort of way and twisted the knob.

McBride laid a hand over hers, opening the door. "Good-night, Mrs. Chandler. Drop in again some time. Any time." He watched her to the turn in the corridor before retiring and closing the door behind him. He felt that he was acquiring a great deal of knowledge that was of no particular use to him. He felt like a farmer with a bumper crop for which there was no possible market. He went to bed.

5

WITH THE MORNING papers came a thermos jug of coffee, all with the compliments of the management and all included at the ridiculously low price of only twenty dollars a day. McBride derived a certain sardonic satisfaction out of the thought of Erin Rourke's face when the expense account was presented.

The papers were all alike in one respect: none of them exactly ignored the war on account of the murder of an obscure man in an even more obscure hotel. Severn and the Hotel Trojan got less than a column, and most of this meager space was devoted to what the police thought. It was disclosed that the police, in the person of Lieutenant Nick Orsatti, had identified Severn with a police record in the name of Seversky, alias this, that and the other. His death was believed to be the result of a gang war. Mr. McGillicuddy was referred to as "the manager." The Trojan was "a local Powell Street hotel." There was no mention whatever of Slugs Foley and his alleged wife Marge, nor of the very tall, very thin man whom the police apparently still thought a figment of McBride's imagination. It seemed that the only actual names fit for print were those of the dead man, of Lieutenant Nick Orsatti, and of the legal occupant of the room, a Rex McBride. The police had not held this Rex McBride, a fact which the papers

hinted was a mistake. The whole thing bore the imprint
of police censorship; indeed McBride felt that the inclusion of his own name was part and parcel of some Machi-
avellian scheme of the toothpick-chewing, derby-hatted
Orsatti. At the moment he could not see that the inclusion
would do him any harm. He lit his second cigarette of the
morning, sipped the very excellent coffee, and reviewed
the rest of the news, frowning considerably over a renewed
outbreak of unexplained accidents in the various war
industries plants up and down the Coast.

The papers hinted darkly of sabotage, and the FBI was
credited with making its usual investigations. The FBI
was another branch of the government service which was
taking McBride's case "under advisement." Though they
had not come right out and said so, it appeared that they
were just a little afraid of McBride. In the first place, he
hadn't gone to Yale—or even Siwash. He was just a guy
who knew his trade, and this too, one felt, was against him.
A private detective worked for money, didn't he? Who
knew, then, but what he would sell out to the enemy? No,
better not to entrust him with a mission such as catching
some little boys with firecrackers saved over from the last
Fourth of July. McBride discovered that he was cursing
rather horribly, even for him and in private, so he stopped
that and got up and went into the bathroom and began
shaving. There was still lather on his face when the telephone rang.

"A Mr. Loeb to see you, Mr. McBride."

"Loeb?"

"Yes sir, a Mr. Sigmund Loeb."

"What does he want?"

"Just a moment, I'll see, sir." After the required moment the clerk downstairs returned to say that Mr. Loeb felt his business with Mr. McBride should remain private, but he would be glad to discuss it first over the telephone. "Shall I have him connected?"

"All right." A trifle absently McBride used the towel about his neck to dab at the drying lather on his cheek. He tried to think of anybody he had ever heard of named Loeb, but all he got was the case in Chicago ten or fifteen years back.

A new voice came to him, quiet but full-bodied and smooth and with the suggestion of oil in it. "Mr. McBride? This is Sigmund Loeb." He paused briefly to laugh, as though amused at a passing thought. "A gentleman I think you know recently approached me with something to sell; something I believe you are interested in. Would you like me to mention that to the police?"

McBride's eyes grew wary. "This gentleman's name?"

"Who knows? The poor fellow had so many."

"You'd better come up," McBride said. He was impelled to bang the phone down and give Mr. Sigmund Loeb an ear-ache, but restrained himself. Some five minutes later when there was a refined knock on the door he had on a terry-cloth robe and his hair was nicely brushed and his teeth shone. In the pocket of the terry-cloth robe was the smaller of his two guns.

Loeb was a rather handsome middle-aged Jew, carefully tailored without being in the least foppish. At first glance, the two most remarkable things about him were his width and his nose. He had quite the widest pair of shoulders McBride had seen in a long time, making him seem shorter than he really was. The nose was not hooked; it was just big, and hawkish and fierce, like an Arab chieftain's. Oddly enough, the eyes on either side of it were gray. Recovering from the fascination of the nose, McBride decided that the eyes were even more remarkable. Humor and intelligence and tolerance lay in them, and in spite of the fierceness of the nose and the subtle threat in the man's words over the phone McBride found himself favorably impressed. He felt that no matter what developed, Mr. Sigmund Loeb would be—if not a valuable ally—at least a worthy antagonist. McBride didn't like pushovers. He was a little ashamed of the gun in his pocket.

Loeb just stood there a moment, hat in his hand and the suggestion of a friendly smile on his wide mobile mouth. "I am not intruding?" His hair was a sort of gun metal streaked with polished pewter.

McBride spoke to the ceiling. "After just threatening me with the cops he asks if he's intruding!"

"That was unfortunate," Loeb said amiably. "What might be termed an exigency of the occasion." He came into the room and even as Delilah Chandler had done made a careful but unobtrusive survey of the entire suite. Satisfied that he and McBride were alone he laid his pearl-gray Homburg on a table, sat and considered McBride with his wide-spaced intelligent eyes. "We need not mince words, you and I, Mr. McBride. The Adelphi necklace has now become something of a liability, yet I am still prepared to buy. It remains but to set a reasonable price, eh?"

McBride was astonished. "You think I've got it?"

"I think it a fairly accurate assumption," Loeb said. "A man whom I knew possessed it is now dead." He made a faint gesture of apology. "Without meaning to give offense I may add that he was found dead in your room." His glance became warmly admiring. "I don't quite know how you managed the police, but I do know that they will find it most interesting if the necklace should turn up in the regular channels—if it is traced back to you." He spread his hands, palms up. "You are known to have been retained to recover the piece. The thief is murdered, and believe me I say that advisedly, Mr. McBride. Had there been a struggle—had you shot him in self-defense, let us say—and then admitted it to the police, things would have been slightly different."

"But I didn't," McBride said. "I slipped him a knife—in the back—and I told the cops it must have been three other guys, so I can't very well give the necklace back to my company without getting clipped for murder."

"Exactly."

McBride was thoroughly angry now, not to mention slightly frightened. This guy Loeb, if he talked, had a party named Rex McBride over the well-known barrel. The Severn-Seversky murder was rapidly assuming terrific proportions. He said, exercising great control, "You're not in too good a spot yourself, Siggy, old pal, old pal. You go to the cops, you'll be admitting you're a fence who was about to buy stolen property. In fact, the cops may even wonder if it wasn't you who stuck the shiv in the guy."

"A possibility," Loeb agreed comfortably. He was not in the least frightened by the prospect. "Of course I have merely to say that the thief *offered* me the stones. I did not buy them."

"And besides," McBride hazarded, "you've got a perfect

alibi for the time Severn was knocked off. You were probably eating cold borsch with the missus and seventeen rabbis."

"They weren't all rabbis," Loeb said.

McBride pointed a triumphant forefinger. "But," he said, "you did not go to the police. You knew the item offered you was stolen, but you did not go to the police." He shook his head sadly. "The boys down at the Hall aren't going to like that. They aren't going to like it a little bit."

Loeb sighed. "It might be embarrassing," he admitted. He brightened. "Better to be embarrassed than gassed, though." He leaned forward, eyes intent on McBride's. "Come now, there is no need for us to discuss the more unpleasant aspects of the affair. Let us just say that you have something for which I offer a ready market and no questions asked." Again he spread his hands in the age-old gesture. "With murder involved I can not now offer quite so much as I had intended, but I will be generous. Say twenty-five thousand dollars."

"Jesus, that's white of you!" McBride sneered. "I'm offering thirty grand myself."

Doubt came into Loeb's eyes. It was gone almost instantly. "Perhaps I could increase the offer." He stood up. "You have another buyer in mind?"

McBride discovered suddenly that he was enjoying himself. There was still the menace of the police, of course, and Mr. Sigmund Loeb could no doubt cause him, McBride, a lot of trouble, but in a bargaining bout McBride felt himself the equal of any fence living. "Before I answer that one, let's talk some more about this guy Severn. He tell you he stole the stuff himself?"

Loeb was pained. "Would he?"

McBride nodded. "No, he probably just found it lying in a gutter. Or some friend of his woke up after a terrific binge, and there it was, right in his pocket." He began pacing the room, the skirts of the terry-cloth robe flapping about his shanks. Outside, a ten o'clock morning sun was trying to dispel the remnants of last night's fog. Through the open windows came the sounds of downtown traffic fourteen stories below. A lone ferryboat's whistle was hoarse and plaintive, mourning the loss of its mates, occasioned by the coming of the bridges. "All right, maybe he didn't tell you everything. He told you something, or you wouldn't have been willing to buy." McBride took the gun out of his pocket and twirled it by its trigger guard. "He wasn't working alone?"

No, Loeb said dryly, he had gathered that Severn-Seversky had had at least one partner, possibly more than one. After showing the merchandise and getting a tentative offer the man had wanted time to think it over. Obviously he had wanted to consult his associates.

"What was the offer?"

"Fifty thousand," Loeb said. "I would have gone higher." Somewhat hastily he added, "Not now, of course. Conditions have changed."

McBride glared at him. "Don't give me that, you chiseler. The rope is worth as much as it ever was. With importations stopped you can cut it up and still make money-even the hundred grand insurance was cheap."

"But now I am risking more," Loeb pointed out genially. "My neck is to me worth several reputations." He looked rather intently at McBride's neck. "I do not know what you value yours at, but a neck and thirty thousand dollars are not to be considered lightly."

McBride disdained comment on this rather too obvious truism. "You happen to know a guy named Slugs Foley?"

Loeb's face became slightly wooden. "I know him."

"How about this guy?" McBride described the lean and cadaverous shadow he had met in the upper hall of the Hotel Trojan.

Startled recognition unhinged Loeb's wooden expression. "The Deacon!" He regarded McBride as though that gentleman had just produced an elephant from his sleeve. "Now that would account for—But no, it couldn't be. The Deacon was just released from San Quentin yesterday. The Adelphi was stolen over a week ago—in Los Angeles."

McBride eyed him with patent disfavor. "Anything I hate, it's a guy that carries on conversations with himself. Just for fun, what would this Deacon account for?

"For the man Severn looking me up in the first place." Mr. Loeb paused to inform McBride that he was not by any means the usual buyer of stolen goods. He was a reputable diamond merchant. He was, he said, possibly the biggest and certainly the most reputable on the Pacific Coast.

"But Severn didn't mention the Deacon—nor Slugs Foley?"

"No."

"Then how come you dealt with him?"

"I hadn't—yet," Loeb pointed out.

"Ever visit him at his hotel?"

Loeb turned that over in his mind several times. Finally he said, "Once." He lifted a hand as McBride would have spoken. "But just once, Mr. McBride, just once. That was when negotiations first began." It became apparent that the interview had taken a turn he did not relish. He rose to his feet. "These things are beside the point. The issue is, do you want to deal with me now or later with the police?"

McBride looked at him speculatively. "I could always shoot you, you know."

"And have another dead body in your room?" Mr. Loeb put on his Homburg at rather a jaunty angle. His large nose twitched with amusement. "I do not think you will, Mr. McBride."

McBride sighed. "You drive a hard bargain, Siggy." Quite suddenly his face became convulsed with rage and he shouted, "Listen, you kike bastard! I haven't got the rocks and I didn't knock anybody off!" More quietly he added, "Not recently, anyway." He pointed the gun at Mr. Loeb's big nose, sighting along the barrel carefully. "Now go on and peddle your wares to the police and see what it gets you."

Loeb was unimpressed. "There's never any hurry about these things, Mr. McBride. Think it over." He went out; behind him the closing door made scarcely a sound.

McBride was still standing there fiddling with the gun when the door opened to admit Detective-Lieutenant Orsatti; indeed it seemed to him impossible that Orsatti had not met Loeb in the hall outside, so short was the elapsed time. Orsatti had not bothered with anything so genteel as a preliminary knock. He just came in. With him was another man in plain clothes, a man who, though he wore neither a toothpick nor a derby, was of the same general type. Orsatti pretended to think McBride was about to shoot him and drew his own gun. "Drop the rod, shamus."

McBride obediently dropped it. His mouth was sullen. "A guy can't even practice being a junior G-Man any more."

Orsatti's toothpick snapped in his teeth. "They want to see you down at the Hall, McBride."

"Why?"

"For one thing," Orsatti said portentously, "the L.A. detective bureau never made that second call you roped us in with." His red-brown eyes were inflamed as though from loss of sleep. "I had an idea they hadn't, so I checked."

McBride was greatly surprised. "Then who did?"

"That's just one of the things we want to talk to you about," Orsatti snarled. He made a gesture to his companion. "Just for fun, give the joint a quick frisk."

"Not without a warrant," McBride said.

"We came prepared for that, too," Orsatti announced. He took the required document from the inside pocket of his baggy serge and tossed it across to McBride. His fat-creased oily skin looked even muddier than it had the night before; the rusty derby a little greener, but McBride was not making the same mistake twice about Orsatti. The guy was dynamite. While the second man ambled inquisitively about the apartment Orsatti replaced the gun in his shoulder clip; a finger and thumb explored a vest pocket and came out with a fresh toothpick to fill the void left by its predecessor. "Any connection between you and the Cyrus H.Q. Chandlers being in the same hotel?"

McBride neither denied nor affirmed the connection. His face was that of an outraged but patient Sioux. "The St. Mark is open to the public, isn't it?"

Orsatti's toothpick slowly traveled the entire width of his mouth. "Seems these Chandlers lost a necklace a week or so back. You wouldn't be working on that, would you?"

McBride shook his head. "We paid off-a hundred grand right on the nose."

"And that ended it?"

"Absolutely."

Orsatti pounced. "Then what are you doing with thirty-five grand in the safe downstairs?"

McBride swore a mental oath to wreak a just and fitting vengeance on the management of the St. Mark for disclosing something that should have been kept sacred from any cops, but especially from these two. He said carefully, "I do what I please with my money."

"It isn't your money!" Orsatti yelled. "It belongs to the Underwriters' Alliance and it was given you to make a buy with." His voice rose even higher, quite a strain on his alcohol-pickled tonsils. "Only you decided to save the dough. You knocked Severn off instead!"

"Did I?"

The other dick came in carrying an armload of McBride's clothes. "Get dressed, mister. We're going down to the Hall."

6

———

OVERLOOKING PORTSMOUTH SQUARE from a window in the Hall of Justice, McBride found little to admire in the view. And Portsmouth Square, regarding the Hall of Justice, seemed to feel the same way. The entire section had a dingy, brooding, almost sullen air—this because of McBride's own unhappy attitude, no doubt—and the Hall especially wore the resentful cloak of the aged and forgotten. It was almost as though the new and quite lovely, if perhaps a bit too pretentious Civic Center, a couple of miles or so away, had deliberately neglected to include a police department of which it was ashamed.

McBride tried hard not to be biased. Indeed, he recalled that until recently the Los Angeles Police Department had had little to boast about. Too, when he was away from San Francisco, the city had charm, a romance utterly lacking in his own home town. It was only when he was actually there and people began pushing him around that he lost the roseate perspective and considered the grime and the packing-box atmosphere. Frequently he had that same cramped outlander's feeling in New York. He wondered if perhaps he weren't just jealous of the tall buildings.

Behind him, the red-haired, red-mustached Captain Wick rustled papers on the battered oak desk. "Now look, McBride, we're doing out best to be reasonable with you, but you've got to come clean." He cleared his throat of some obstruction. "A man has been killed. It is almost a foregone conclusion that it was over a division of loot, or something of the sort."

McBride turned. "Why?"

Orsatti said in an enraged voice, "If you say 'why' just once more I'm going to kick your teeth in."

There was another man present, a slight middle-aged man who looked something like Mr. McGillicuddy and was distressed by Orsatti's uncouth remarks. He wore pince-nez. He was an assistant prosecuting attorney. "If I may say so, the 'why' is quite obvious, Mr. McBride. You were retained to investigate the theft of a certain necklace, insured by Underwriters' Alliance. We are led to believe that you followed the Cyrus H.Q. Chandlers to Seattle, and back down here to San Francisco. It seems quite apparent that this interest stems from their loss; in other words, you suspected them of complicity in the theft."

McBride nodded. "All right, I'll come clean with you." He looked at Orsatti. "I'd have done it before if certain parties hadn't had to throw their weight—and their fists— around." He wondered how his own fist would fit the fat and unlovely jaw of Lieutenant Orsatti. He postponed finding out. "I did think it was an inside job. So did the L.A. police, though they were unwilling to antagonize important people like the Chandlers by saying so. Also, they weren't able to get around as freely as a private op." He lit a cigarette and snapped the match out the open window into Kearney Street. "Now I'll tell you why I thought it was an inside job. There were marks of illegal entry into the Chandler apartment, but they were pretty clumsy. Besides that, nothing was taken but the Adelphi necklace. There were a lot of other things around; things that would have been a great deal easier to peddle, but the thief or thieves just ignored them." He was unsuccessful in his attempt to blow a smoke ring. "To me it didn't seem reasonable."

"You seem to be speaking almost exclusively in the past tense," the assistant prosecutor observed. "Are we to conclude that your beliefs have changed? Something has occurred, no doubt, to convince you that your suspicions of the Chandlers were unjustified?"

"I wouldn't say that." McBride shrugged. "I'd say rather that nothing had occurred—nothing whatever. In almost ten days of reasonably close surveillance I've been able to find no corroborative evidence."

Captain Wick rustled some more papers. Orsatti seemed about to say something, but didn't. The prosecutor said tiredly, "Very well, now we come to the matter of the murdered man in your room—Seversky. Are we to believe that was merely coincidence?"

"I don't care what you believe," McBride said flatly. "Coincidence is something that only authors are supposed to avoid. The rest of us can't help ourselves." He deliberately dropped his cigarette on the scarred linoleum floor and crushed it out with his foot. "I can get you the cab driver who picked me up at the station and hauled me all over hell-and-gone looking for a hotel that wasn't full up. He'll tell you that it was he who suggested the Trojan, not me."

Captain Wick said, "We've already found the—"

"Well, for Christ's sake!" Orsatti shouted. "Go on, tell him everything. Tell him—"

"Orsatti!" Wick said sharply.

McBride said with an affection of Christian forbearance, "It's all right, Captain. I've been persecuted by tougher monkeys than him."

Orsatti seemed in imminent danger of a stroke. "Explain the thirty-five grand in the St. Mark safe, then!"

"I already have," McBride said. He looked at the prosecutor. "The cops in Los Angeles will tell you I'm something of a gambler. I always carry a roll, just in case."

The gentleman addressed took off his pince-nez and pointed them at McBride's chest. "Tell me, Mr. McBride, isn't it a practice of insurance detectives actually to consort with the thieves; to buy back stolen articles at a fraction of their insured value and thus minimize the loss?"

"I wouldn't know," McBride said. He winked at Captain Wick. "Offhand, I'd say that was a leading question." He returned his attention to the prosecutor. "I'd say the procedure you've outlined would require a great deal of skill and entail terrific risks, wouldn't you? A man caught at it would certainly find himself in a jam with the law."

"Like you are now," Orsatti said.

"Oh, no," McBride said. He decided he was tired of standing and selected a chair, sat in it and stretched his legs out in front of him. "Suppose I were actually the type of man you describe. Suppose that this Severn—or Seversky—had actually stolen the Adelphi and that I knew it. Would I kill him, in my own room, and then lie to the police about it? Wouldn't that prohibit my ever returning the necklace to its rightful owners?"

"It wouldn't prohibit you from selling it to some fence and getting your company's money back," Orsatti said angrily.

"True," McBride said. He showed his teeth in something that if it were supposed to be a smile was certainly a nasty one. "And the first time you find me doing anything as silly as that you can toss me in the can and throw the key away." He stood up violently. "God damn it, a guy like me has got two choices! He can either catch his man fair and square, recover the junk and prosecute, or he can make a deal. If he makes a deal, that's got to be fair and square too, or the word gets around and he never gets a chance to make another one." He spread his hands. "If I had done what you guys think I did, I'd have every crook in the United States laying for me from now on."

The prosecutor said gently, "A guy like you, Mr. McBride?"

"A guy like I'm supposed to be."

"I see." The man with the pince-nez polished them a trifle absently and replaced them on his nose. "This— ummm—Slugs Foley and his wife. Have you any suggestions regarding them?"

"No."

"I take it you are aware that he too, has a record?"

"He looked like the kind of guy that would have," McBride admitted. "I told that to Wick and Orsatti last night." He did not again refer to the tall thin man whom he knew now to be the Deacon and to have a record as long as either Severn or Slugs Foley. He could not very well reveal the source of his knowledge without incriminating Mr. Sigmund Loeb, a gentleman who could either be a very great menace or a very great asset, depending on the circumstances. He said, "Why don't you look up the

Foleys, Orsatti, instead of spending all your time on me? At least I haven't tried to run out."

Orsatti's eyes flamed. "When I want your advice I'll ask for it!"

"Well, sure," McBride said equably. He picked up his hat, a twenty-dollar Knox which he thought looked very well on him. "If it's the reward you fellows are worrying about, all you've got to do is produce the stuff. My company always pays off." He pretended to think that it was really not the reward at all that they were interested in. He stared pointedly at Orsatti's chin. "Remember that, Lieutenant; we always pay off." He smiled at Captain Wick and the assistant prosecutor. "May I go now?"

"The inquest is Monday," Wick said gruffly.

"I'll be around," McBride promised. He went out.

There was a bright-looking young man loitering across the street. There was another, almost his twin, down the block in a car parked beside a fire plug. McBride thought he recalled seeing the same two outside the Hotel St. Mark when he had emerged in the company of Lieutenant Orsatti and partner. He did not think they had been following Orsatti. He wondered if perhaps these weren't the "assistants" ascribed to him by that champion of ladies in distress, Rodriguez Franz Sebastian. He crossed the street diagonally and apparently without purpose, ignoring the foot-loiterer and pausing when he reached the opposite sidewalk to get out a package of cigarettes, select one and return the others to his pocket. It appeared that he was unable to find a match, though. He was still looking for one when he came alongside the parked car. He addressed its occupant. "Got a match?"

The young man looked a little flustered. He had the bluest eyes and the freshest, pinkest skin McBride had ever encountered in the male of the species. "Why-why, yes, I believe I have." He produced one and tried not to look too fascinated as McBride lit the cigarette.

McBride exhaled a great cloud of smoke and watched it drift away in the wind. Obviously McBride had nothing more important to do than engage a chance acquaintance in conversation. "Nice day."

"It certainly is, isn't it?" There was a brief hiatus.

"Yes, it certainly is."

The young man on foot, the one up the block a ways, began drifting down. McBride said pleasantly, "Anything in particular you wanted to know about me?"

Some of the pinkness left the first young man's face. He avoided McBride's eye. "No."

"I thought there might me," McBride said. He stepped backward into the path of the drifter. There was a mild collision. "Oh, pardon me!"

"Got a match?" the newcomer said. Close up, he looked like an All-American blocking back. He had neither cigar, cigarette nor pipe. Perhaps he wanted the match to whittle. The young man in the car, sighing a little, produced a second match. Up the street Lieutenant Orsatti and his burly companion came out of Police Headquarters and got into a car. McBride waved at them as they went past. He looked ingenuously from one to the other of his new-found friends. "Feds?"

The one on foot said, "Feds—what's that?"

The other one said disgustedly, "Save it, Jerry, he's wise."

He moved over a little farther under the wheel. "Maybe we'd better take a little ride, chum."

"Is this a pinch?"

The blocking back crowded McBride. "No." Now that his companion had suggested a definite line of action he seemed capable of cooperation. McBride got in the car.

7

MR. W. PATRICK was a stoutish, moderately competent-looking man whose function seemed to be the direction of quite a lot of precocious children similar to the
two who had brought McBride in. He was dressed well
but inconspicuously in several shades of brown; indeed he
himself ran to browns: skin, hair and eyes reminded you of
those panels in Chamber-of-Commerce lobbies labeled:
"This panel constructed of woods native to this state."
McBride knew the brown man's name was W. Patrick
because it had said so on the door. He knew that W. Patrick
must have something on the ball because in spite of his
quiet manner the bright young men all seemed scared as
hell of him.

There was a desk in the room, and three chairs and
quite an array of steel filing cabinets. The windows looked
out and down upon Civic Center. W. Patrick sat in one
of the chairs; the one behind the desk. McBride sat in
another. The two young men were apparently disinclined
to sit down at all, so the third chair remained empty. W.
Patrick said, "What is your interest in the Chandlers, Mr.
McBride?"

McBride was intrigued with the way the sun glinted on
the dome of City Hall. "What's yours?"

One of the young men, the blocking back, made a

fist of his right hand and looked intently at McBride's mouth. Mr. Patrick said, "Maybe you'd better wait outside, Jerry." Without looking at Jerry's partner he said, "Maybe you'd better wait outside too, Kim." When they had gone he bent and pulled out a lower drawer of the desk, swiveled halfway around and put his neat brown shoes on the open drawer. His neat brown eyes considered McBride carefully. "The boys interfering in your business?"

"Some," McBride said.

"But you don't care to state your business?"

"I don't mind," McBride said. He got out his card case and tossed it across the desk. The case contained his personal cards, his business cards, his license and gun permits. "The Chandlers lost something. I thought they might have found it again and forgotten to mention it."

"Hmmmm," W. Patrick said. "This is very interesting."

"Why?" This seemed to be McBride's season for asking that question. He hoped that somebody might get around to answering it. He felt that it was hardly cricket for so many people to know so much that he didn't know. He was beginning to believe that he was not so good a detective as he had thought.

"Cyrus H.Q. Chandler is a very important man," W. Patrick observed presently. "I hardly think that—"

"You'd be surprised how many important people I meet in my business," McBride said. In his voice was the trace of a sneer. "Sometimes I'm practically overwhelmed." He leaned forward. "Now take you, for instance. I'll bet your job is to see that no Jap spies sit in on any of Mr. Chandler's conferences; or that he doesn't go out without his rubbers."

The brown man denied that he was important. "Nothing

is important any more except that we win this war." There
was neither affection nor dislike in the intent stare he
turned on McBride's face. "Mr. Chandler himself is unim-
portant—as an individual. The work he is doing is not. It
is my business to see that nothing interferes with it—not
even you, Mr. McBride."

"Meaning that I am to lay off?" McBride got up and put
both hands flat on the desk. His dark eyes had a curiously
muddy look. "Listen, Mr. W. Patrick, I'll give you odds that
that suggestion came from Cyrus H.Q. Chandler himself."

"What makes you think that, Mr. McBride?"

"He threatened to take steps," McBride said. "This is
one of them." His mouth was hard and unpleasant. "I don't
like that, Mr. W. Patrick. I don't like it a little bit. It smacks
too much of the kind of thing that's hamstringing Thurman Arnold, and believe me I hold no brief for Thurman
Arnold either."

For the first time since the interview began the brown
man's eyes showed a glint of humor. "You're referring, no
doubt, to certain indictments that have been quashed for
the duration."

"And will never be permitted to raise their ugly heads
again," McBride said nastily. "By the time this war is over
all will be forgotten." He looked for and found his hat.
"Well, this is one indictment that won't be, by God! I had
almost given up the Chandlers as a possibility; this practically confirms my original theory." He put the hat on,
carefully, as though it were the most important thing in
the world that he get it just right. "Chandler doesn't want
me snooping around. If he didn't have something to worry
about he wouldn't give a damn. Therefore I'll continue to

snoop and I'll thank you to keep your sophomore halfbacks out from under my feet."

"Young man of violence," W. Patrick said musingly. "Seems to me I've heard of you before—somewhere." He had not risen from the desk, nor did he now look directly at McBride. "Wasn't there an affair— Oh, yes, in Honolulu, wasn't it?"

If McBride were surprised his face didn't show it. "That's just a case in point," he said angrily. "I damn near lost two hundred thousand dollars trying to be a patriot."

"But you didn't," W. Patrick said.

"No thanks to the FBI," McBride sneered. "A friend of mine, a stumble-bum ex-prizefighter, broke that one."

Mr. Patrick nodded. "Well, it's been a pleasure meeting you, Mr. McBride." From a drawer of the desk he got out a folder of papers and began leafing through them. "If you learn anything further let me know, will you?"

"No."

"First," W. Patrick said.

"The hell with you!" McBride shouted. He banged out, knowing that somewhere—somehow—W. Patrick had made a monkey out of him. He hoped that Jerry, the blocking back, or the blue-eyed, pink-skinned Kim would try to stop him, but they were nowhere in sight. A lot of other bright young men were at desks in the outer office, but they paid McBride no more attention than if he were the gutter-bred news kid he had once been. In a bar on McAllister Street he had three straight ryes, one right after the other.

He was in an excellent mood for a fight when he called for Susan, to take her to lunch. He found that Susan already had a swain. It was a Saturday afternoon and the offices of Stilton, Kramm & Dutcher were just closing. In the reception room Mr. Arthur McGillicuddy fiddled with his hat and eyed McBride without love. "Susan is lunching with me," he said. He seemed to have recovered from his fainting spell of the night before. He looked pretty good. Behind thick lenses his eyes were definitely antagonistic. He had a red carnation in his buttonhole.

Susan came out of an inner office, putting on her gloves. She wore a green wool suit and a pair of silver foxes. A rakish wide-brimmed hat, her under-arm purse, gloves, shoes and stockings were silver-gray, to match the foxes. If McBride were any judge—and he thought he was—the outfit must have set her back several hundred dollars. He must, he decided, investigate the possibilities of certified public accountancy. Susan looked from McBride to Mr. McGillicuddy with pretty dismay. "Oh, my goodness!"

McBride glared at her. "Does the line form at the right?"

"I'm so sorry." She seemed really to be. "Arthur, would you mind very much if—if we sort of made a party of it? Mr. McBride—"

"No," Mr. McGillicuddy said firmly. His somewhat receding chin indicated an unexpected stubbornness. "I've already engaged a table—for two—out at the Beach."

McBride felt uncomfortably like an adolescent who has been stood up at a junior prom. The rye in him said that he should bust this panty-waist McGillicuddy in the nose. Susan's eyes said that if he did she would never speak to him again. He bowed with exaggerated gallantry. "Enjoy yourselves, children."

Fuming, he departed and ate a solitary lunch in

Helmuth's on Ellis Street. He was on his third stein of beer and dissecting his second pig's knuckle when he discovered that Mr. Rodriguez Sebastian of the Para Consulate liked German food too. Sebastian discovered McBride at about the same time. They glared at each other across half a dozen intervening tables at which half a dozen parties were being pretty noisy. Helmuth's was popular.

Finally Sebastian said something to his waiter, got up and came over. He was quite handsome in double-breasted gray flannels. His mustache could have been drawn on with a black pencil. "You wouldn't be following me, would you?" He accented the "me" slightly, calling attention to the fact that he had warned McBride against further annoying the Chandler ladies.

McBride gnawed at a pig's knuckle. "Why should I be?"

"Have you seen Celeste this morning?"

"No."

"She seems to have disappeared," Sebastian said.

McBride wiped his fingers daintily on a corner of the tablecloth. "All right, I'll confess. I threw her in the bay." He appeared to reflect on the circumstances. "Up around Carquinez Straits, I think it was." He wondered what Sebastian would do if informed that the "assistants" were Feds. He decided he would be mean and not tell him.

"You're really not very funny, you know," Sebastian said. His handsome velvet eyes reminded McBride of something that had to do with mailed fists. "Delilah is worried."

"No!"

"Delilah visited you in your rooms last night," Sebastian said. It was a statement of fact.

McBride was noncommittal. "Did she?" His eyes glowed

as though at a memory. "That babe can visit me any time she wants to." He was quite prepared when Sebastian swung at him; in fact he already had the beer stein in his hand. He hit Sebastian smack on the chin with the stein, and Sebastian went down, pulling the tablecloth and all the dishes on top of him with a tremendous clatter. McBride discovered that there was a little beer left in the stein. He emptied it over Sebastian's oblivious face, as though trying to revive him. "He fell," he explained to the startled assemblage. Three or four waiters bent solicitously over the stricken man. McBride laid a bill beside his stein on the denuded table. "I think he has high blood pressure." He went out, shaking his head as though surprised that Helmuth's would serve intoxicants to people with high blood pressure.

On the sidewalk he chose a cab with a deliberate eye for the toughest-looking driver. He showed the driver Sean O'Hara's card. "Know where that is?"

"Sure."

A policeman came rather hurriedly around the corner and went into Helmuth's. McBride got into the cab. "All right, prove it." They went away.

Bowling down the Peninsula toward Burlingame McBride considered the back of the hacker's neck and some of the more curious aspects of the Chandler case as related to the Adelphi necklace. It was curious, for instance, that the lovely though somewhat aloof Delilah should have softened to the extent of baring her jealousy to one Rex McBride. He did not doubt her jealousy, nor that—considering Celeste—she had a sound reason for it. The point was, why now, instead of, say, ten days ago? The answer to that seemed to be that Delilah didn't care so much about the seduction of her own husband as she did about the possible seduction of Mr. Rodriguez Franz Sebastian. What was it Delilah had called him? Roddy, that was it. Yes, it seemed safe to assume that Delilah was not above a little off-side seduction herself, and resented competition from her adopted daughter. She resented it so much that she was willing to hint to McBride that perhaps, after all, Celeste had stolen the Adelphi.

But suppose you discounted the jealousy angle, say ninety per cent? Suppose indeed that it had been Delilah who filched her own necklace? Even without the jealousy motive she might find it expedient to throw the blame on her synthetic offspring. Something might have occurred which had put the fear of God into her. McBride recalled that Delilah had appeared to recognize Sean O'Hara, there in the Stardust Room last night. There was no doubt at all that Celeste had recognized him. Hence, McBride felt, Sean O'Hara must know things about both ladies that he himself did not know. He would not, of course, be able to ask O'Hara about these things directly. He would have to pretend that he wanted further details about the projected Nevada enterprise. Too, there was the matter of Slugs Foley. Had O'Hara managed to pick up anything about the Slug and been unable to contact McBride? Either of these approaches would serve as an entering wedge.

As a matter of fact, McBride was genuinely interested in Slugs Foley and wife; he was only slightly less interested in the very tall, very thin man called the Deacon. He had it on the excellent authority of no less a personage than Mr. Sigmund Loeb that the Adelphi had actually been in the possession of that two-time loser Seversky. Indeed, come to think of it, Severn-Seversky was now a three-time loser, death being even more final than life imprisonment. So Seversky had had the necklace. In the same hotel with him had been Slugs Foley and Marge and the Deacon. It was reasonable to suppose that all three had been working together, or that one or more had been preying upon the others. McBride felt that a meeting with any one of those left alive was to be desired, if for no other reason than that the producing the killer of Seversky would remove Detective-lieutenant Orsatti from his neck.

Thinking about Orsatti reminded him of the brown man in the Federal Building. It was obvious that Mr. W. Patrick was concerned about any possible scandal attaching to a government big-wig. On general principles McBride disapproved of this tendency, but what with the rye and the beer and the wholly satisfactory pig's knuckles he was in an expansive mood. He would forgive the brown man.

Thinking of pig's knuckles reminded him of his own, which remained unscathed because of the miraculous properties of a beer stein. He wondered if Roddy Sebastian would swear out an assault-and-battery complaint. He thought not. Roddy might challenge him, McBride, to a duel; he might even stick a knife in McBride's back, but he would not cry to the cops.

The hacker now felt that he was far enough out of town so that he could confide some pertinent information about the place they were going. "I forgot to tell you it ain't open at this time o' day."

"Like hell, you forgot!" McBride said. He saw that there

was already two-seventy on the meter. They were just passing through San Bruno. "Who gave you that cauliflower?"

Far from being offended the hacker seemed actually
pleased by the interest his abnormal ear had provoked.
"Well, I'll tell you, chum. I could claim it was Packy
McFarlane, just before I laid him out in the twennieth.
I could even say it was Dempsey. But the fact is, chum, it
was a cop. There was two other cops holding me," he added
modestly, "and the cop that hit me had a chair arm; but
still and all I ain't one to claim no laurels I don't deserve."

"I can see that," McBride said. He was impressed. He
said, "One thing I like about you, it's your utter honesty."
He stared significantly at the meter which now read three-
ten. "Imagine not waiting till we were all the way there
before you remembered."

"I could've," the hacker pointed out.

"That's what I mean," McBride said. "Even such dubious
honesty as yours is better than none at all."

The hacker cocked an eye at him by way of the rear-vi-
sion mirror. "You mean like coming outa that joint back
there just before the beat cop ran in?"

"Something like that," McBride conceded. He did not
bother to deny what his charioteer obviously believed:
that Helmuth's had lost the contents of their cash register.
"What's your name, chum? I don't mean the one on your
license there. What do they call you?"

"Butch."

"Unique."

The red neck turned an angry magenta. "Is that a crack,
pally?" The cab slowed appreciably. "On account of if it is,

and irregardless I been hit plenty times below the belt, I still got all my faculties and I can lick any man says I ain't."

"Sure you can," McBride said.

Butch was not to be detoured by so obvious an evasion. "Well, have I or haven't I?"

McBride appeared puzzled. "Haven't you what?"

"Got all my faculties!"

"How do I know?" McBride demanded. He held his breath while three other drivers avoided an imminent collision with the cab. "And anyway, unique doesn't mean what you think. It means outstanding—different."

Butch was only partially mollified. "Well, if them guys ain't different I don't know what is."

McBride sighed. "Forget it, Butch."

"Well, sure, but—"

"Forget it."

Butch relapsed into sullen silence and once more concentrated on his driving. McBride looked out the window at the flow of Saturday afternoon traffic. The liquor was dying in him and he was suddenly oppressed with the feeling that he was the hare instead of the hound in this chase. His mind returned to Orsatti; to Captain Wick and the assistant prosecutor. He hadn't been kidding them when he'd said his life wouldn't be worth a bent nickel if word got around that he'd knifed in the back a man he'd been dealing with. Any gun on the Pacific Coast would regard him as fair game. He decided that from now on he had better keep a watchful eye out for casual bushwhackers.

After a time Butch said, "You a stranger in the city?"

"Sort of."

"Use a cab much?"

McBride roused a little. "At your prices?"

"Well, that's what I mean," Butch said. "A guy that's a right guy, I could maybe shade the meter a little. I ain't no hog, and if you was to give me a buzz instead of just asking the dispatcher for a cab—" He left the suggestion hanging. "You working for O'Hara's syndicate?"

"Unh-hunh."

"I hear somebody knocked over a joint of theirs down in Los."

McBride was not visibly impressed by this information. "I'm glad to know you can read. It was in the papers."

"That ain't where I got it, pally."

McBride sat up a little straighter. "You wouldn't happen to have heard who did it, would you?"

"No."

McBride relaxed. "Jesus, what a let-down you build up to!"

"But I might hear of something," Butch persisted.

McBride sighed. "Well, if you ever do—and it isn't in the papers first—look me up. The name is McBride and I'm at the St. Mark."

"Okay, pally."

Perhaps a mile beyond Burlingame a lateral highway turned in toward the hills, and presently the cab swung from this into a narrow, steeply climbing secondary road, oiled but not paved. Patches of scrub and live oaks were interspersed with well-tended olive groves, and here and there rhododendrons bloomed riotously. The air was clean and fresh and crystal clear. It was a fine day.

The cab passed through a pair of gateposts linked by a weathered overhead sign which said this was El Rancho

Verdugo. Gravel rattled against the under side of the fenders and Butch said, "Well, this is it. Like I told you, it ain't open."

There was a pretty big parking area, solidly fenced with overgrown palms. The house rose from a shrub-dotted lawn which had been allowed to get a little out of hand. It was a big place, and impressive after the manner of the early 1900s; lots of unnecessary gables and gingerbread. In broad daylight it had the weathered, slightly decayed look of the sign over the gateposts. At night it would probably look like something your fairy godmother brought you, for there was a lot of outside wiring strung with colored light bulbs. McBride wondered why all night clubs had to look so lousy in the daytime. They always reminded him unpleasantly of hangovers.

He got out of the cab and went up the circular drive to a broad painted wooden porch which creaked a little under his weight. The front door was locked and nobody answered his knock. He went along the porch, shielding his eyes from the sun and peering into windows. Those that weren't shuttered showed him the usual dance floor surrounded by tables too close together, an orchestra shell and a ceiling draped with inverted undulant billows of colored gauze. The tables were all set up. Some of them had reserved signs on them.

McBride tried hammering on the door once more, got nowhere and was on the point of giving it up as a bad job when almost under his feet, it seemed, there was the sharp crash of glass. He ran down off the porch and met Butch coming up the drive. "You bust a window?"

"No."

They ran around the nearest corner of the house and were just in time to see the lady who had broken a window come crawling out of it. It was a basement half-window and quite small, but the lady was determined and just drunk enough to ignore bits of impedimenta like shattered glass and one thing and another. She was mumbling, "I'll show'm, I'll show the bastards," over and over again, and she seemed quite unaware that she had an audience. She was Celeste Chandler.

A man came around from the rear of the house, a big, lumbering hulk of a man, rubbing sleep out of his eyes with one hand and juggling a gun with the other. His eyes focused on the erratically weaving figure of Celeste and he yelled, "Hey, you!" and lifted the gun, thought better of it and began to stalk her. Somewhere Celeste had lost one of her high heels and this and the load she was carrying gave her movements the uncertainty of direction a twin-motored plane has when one of the engines suddenly dies.

She and the guy with the gun became conscious of the taxi at the same time. From that it was but a step till they became conscious of Butch and McBride. To Celeste the cab was the more important. She went sailing off toward it. The guy with the gun turned it on McBride, ignoring Butch, because in spite of the movies it is practically impossible to point a gun at two people at once. McBride stood perfectly still, fascinated by the gun but even more fascinated by Celeste's progress toward the cab.

Something white and round and apparently very solid hurtled into his range of vision and clunked the gun-toter alongside the head. He dropped like a poled steer in a slaughterhouse. Amazed by these phenomena, McBride

turned and discovered Butch in the act of lifting another
white-painted cobblestone from a flower border. "Never
mind," McBride said.

He went chasing after Celeste who had just found out
she couldn't start the cab, because Butch had the keys in
his pocket. McBride could hear her cursing from fifty
feet away. She was still threatening to show somebody
something. "I'll show those bastards!" She got out of the
cab, stumbled and fell to her hands and knees in the loose
gravel.

McBride fell on her. "All right, baby, take it easy. We're
friends."

She relaxed instantly. Her body became as loose and
flaccid and inert as a possum's surrounded by hounds. The
possum illusion was carried still further as McBride hauled
her erect and saw the shine of her eyes between lids that
were almost tight shut but not quite. She was a very disheveled young woman, but she was not unconscious. McBride
shook her. "Remember me, baby?"

Her eyes fluttered open, the sleeping princess awakened
by her knight. "McBride?"

"Very charming," McBride said, "but you can quit acting
now." He leaned her against the side of the cab. "Or would
you rather I threw you back in the dungeon?"

She licked her lips. There was plenty of liquor on her
breath but there was something else, too. McBride thought
that somebody must have fed her a Mickey. "No," she said,
gagging a little at the taste in her mouth. "Take me back
to town, McBride?"

"All right." He put her in the cab.

Butch Larsen came strolling up, very smug in the knowledge that he had performed like a hero and admiring his adversary's gun which he had taken as a trophy. "How much you think I can get for this in a hock-shop, pally?"

"You'd better keep it," McBride advised him. He looked up the slope to where the gorilla still lay as he had fallen. "Or did you kill the guy?"

Butch denied that he had killed anybody. "You could use that chump's head to bowl with." He carefully avoided looking at Celeste but he could not resist a frozen-lipped inquiry. "Who's the broad?"

"Friend of mine," McBride said. He saw that there was blood on the palms of his hands. Celeste had not come through the shattered window unscathed. "Let's go back home, chum. The St. Mark." He got into the cab beside the girl and they started. After a while she began to cry, not noisily. McBride put an arm around her and pillowed her head on his shoulder. "Anything you want to tell me, baby?"

She clung to him. "Not now." Presently she lifted her head and showed him her eyes. "Could you—could we please not talk about it yet, McBride?"

"If you like."

"Not to anybody?"

"If you like," he said again. His face was wooden.

She sighed, like a very small, very tired child, and relaxed in his arms. "I can be nice to people I like, McBride."

"Sure."

"Make me like you."

"All right." He used his free hand to smooth the damp ringlets of hair from her forehead. Mascara had smudged her cheeks a little beneath the heavy, dark lashes. She was quite lovely. They were almost into the city before she spoke again. "I didn't take it, McBride." It was obvious that she meant the Adelphi necklace.

He shook his head as though annoyed at the interruption to his thoughts. "What has O'Hara got on you?"

She shivered. "I—I owe him some money."

"What was he trying to do—take it out in trade?"

Her voice was small and muffled against his chest. "Yes."

They came in on Market Street and presently turned up the hill on Mason, crossing over a couple of blocks up to the side entrance of the hotel. In the lobby they came face to face with Delilah and Rodriguez Sebastian. Celeste apparently had reached the end of her strength. She swayed against McBride, clinging to him tightly. Her voice was for his ear alone. "Don't tell him!"

McBride pushed her into Sebastian's arms. "She had an accident."

"You must be careful that you don't have one, too," Sebastian said evenly. Something had changed his handsome velvet eyes to jet, cold and hard and calculating. He and Celeste and Delilah got into an elevator and were lifted from sight.

8

THERE WAS A slip in McBride's mail box which said that a Mr. Erin Rourke had telephoned and would call again about five o'clock. McBride rode up to his rooms and waited for it. Reflecting on the manner in which he and Butch Larsen had rescued a damsel in distress,—and there was no doubt that Celeste had actually been in distress—an excruciatingly funny idea occurred to him. Suppose Delilah, jealous to the point of desperation, had enlisted Sean O'Hara to help her get rid of Celeste? And suppose that Celeste suspected as much, and was planning to get even. This would account for a lot of things, notably Celeste's unwillingness to talk about details.

There were, unfortunately, too many arguments against this theory, however. For one thing, Sean O'Hara was not the type of man to be casually employed in a feud which did not concern him personally. Some of his gorillas might be interested in picking up a bit of side money, but not O'Hara himself. Too, Celeste's story that she owed O'Hara money was credible enough. There is nothing that a gambler, even a big-time gambler, hates more than a welsher, and it was perfectly possible that because of Celeste's position she had been allowed to get into O'Hara for an amount which even he would take certain risks in order to collect. McBride was ready to discount by at least fifty per cent O'Hara's intent to, as he himself had put it, take the debt out in trade. O'Hara might be willing to exert pressure; to put the fear of God into the girl; but he would not be willing to accept her favors in lieu of cash. Not if the cash ran to any sizable amount, as it must in order to induce the syndicate to go to extremes. No, try as he would, McBride could not visualize the fat man as the wolf of the ten-twent'-thirt' meller-drammers.

Thinking of wolves brought McBride around to that South American diplomat, that representative of a Never-Never Land called Para, Mr. Rodriguez Franz Sebastian. Why had Celeste insisted that McBride not tell Sebastian about O'Hara? It was almost as though Sebastian, *especially*, was to be kept in the dark. Why?

Again McBride recalled various incidents during his and Susan's dinner last night in the Stardust Room. Celeste had done her utmost to keep Sebastian and O'Hara apart; she did not want Sebastian aware that she even knew O'Hara. Obviously she was afraid of both, but as a choice of two evils she was ready to take O'Hara. Why? And what, in Christ's name, did any of the recent developments have to do with the stolen Adelphi necklace? If anything.

Sighing, McBride gave it up as he would a particularly complicated—indeed any—crossword puzzle and went into the bath to wash Celeste's blood off his hands. One thing was certain, he was adhering to the McBride tradition—a species of crime detection known as lighting a fire under the pot and watching it boil over. This method was apt to be a little messy sometimes, not so admirable as the more intellectual deduction and induction, but in his case it frequently had been effective.

The telephone rang. It was the astute Mr. Erin Rourke calling from Los Angeles. Rourke was deeply wounded at McBride's neglect. "What am I supposed to do, guess where you are all the time?"

"You're a pretty good guesser," McBride said. He thought of something. "Which reminds me, that trick you pulled last night didn't fool the dicks for more than half an hour. A fat and greasy and particularly obnoxious one named Orsatti took the trouble to check back and find out that you weren't the L.A. chief of dicks, after all."

Rourke had a brief moment of worry, because impersonating an officer, even over the telephone, is not a nice thing to be convicted of; especially is it not nice for the respected vice-president of a big corporation to be convicted of. "Does he know who it was?"

"I don't know," McBride said. "That's just one of the things he left sort of hanging in the air. It gives him an excuse for calling on me again." He described Orsatti's morning visit and the ensuing grilling down at the Hall of Justice. "Because of the circumstances of the Seversky kill he had enough to swing a search warrant. He knows I'm carrying thirty-five grand. So does his chief, and an assistant prosecutor. They don't think it's my mad money." He gnawed a trifle absently on a knuckle. "In fact they think it was to make a buy with; only they think I got Scotch all of a sudden and killed the guy instead."

"Then this Seversky really did have something to do with the theft?"

"It's beginning to look that way," McBride admitted. "He and this Slugs Foley you dug up and another guy who may or may not know what it's all about. You learn anything else about Foley from the cops down there?"

"He isn't a jewel man," Rourke said. "Previous convictions have been for heists and straight gun work."

McBride thought about that for a moment. Presently he said, "Just for fun you might see what you can get on a party known as the Deacon." He described the tall thin man who had the manner of an undertaker's assistant. "I don't know his real name, though I can probably find out. He was sprung from San Quentin yesterday or the day before, so it isn't possible he was in on the original heist. Just for fun, though—"

"You know what I think?" Rourke demanded. "I think you're fumbling around in the dark. I think you don't know what you're doing. I think—"

McBride cursed him. "I don't care what you think. Just quit calling me up, that's all. I've got enough troubles."

Rourke's voice got a sly, insinuating quality. "Isn't there a woman mixed up in it somewhere?"

"Sure," McBride said, "two of them. Delilah and Celeste Chandler."

"I didn't mean those," Rourke said. "An informant mentioned something about a—a bookkeeper, isn't she? A very lovely bookkeeper?"

"So you've been spying on me!"

Rourke was smug. "Oh, I wouldn't say that, my boy. I was just worried about you, that's all." After a moment he said, "Miss Ford was worried about you, too. Especially after she heard about the bookkeeper."

"You keep her out of this!" McBride yelled. He meant Kay Ford, to whom he was more or less engaged to be married. "I won't have her sticking her nose in, nor you either, you—you Fagin!"

"Just like a sailor," Rourke observed sadly. "A girl in every port." He disconnected.

"The trouble with you," McBride shouted, though it was obvious Rourke could not hear him, "you're afraid I might actually have to lay out some of that thirty-five grand!"

A cool voice said in his ear, "Will you repeat that number, pul-lease?"

"Thirty-five grand!" And then, grinning at himself, "Don't try to find that one in the phone book, sister." He replaced the phone with exaggerated care.

It was odd that it should ring again almost instantly and that it should be Susan, whom he had practically denied knowing. Her voice was just as lovely as ever. "Are you still angry with me?"

"No."

"Well, you don't sound very pleased, either."

"Oh, but I am," he assured her gallantly. "I'm pleased positively no end."

"Now you're being sarcastic." She seemed disappointed in him. "Would you like to have dinner with me?"

He hesitated. "Is that an invitation or a hint?"

"No, I owe you one for last night. Besides, I really had promised Mr. McGillicuddy to go to lunch with him. I forgot. Besides, I thought it would be a grand opportunity to ask him about the people living at the Trojan, and you said you were interested. Besides—"

"Well, what?"

"I've already bought the steak," Susan said. She described

it in detail. "It's such a lovely steak, and if I rubbed it just the littlest bit with garlic—"

McBride discovered that he was ravenous, but he held out for one more thing. "Would there be some stout, too? Or say some half-and-half?"

"If you brought it, there would."

"And would you go riding with me afterward?" He had in mind going out to O'Hara's again, hoping that Butch Larsen's estimate of the guard's head had been wrong. But even if the cobblestone hadn't killed the guy it certainly ought to have affected his memory. "I feel kind of lucky tonight and there's a place down the Peninsula."

"All right," Susan said. "Bring some French rolls too, will you?"

McBride was outraged. "Well, for Christ's sake! Are you sure you've got the steak?"

"Good-by now," Susan said. "Remember to tell the man you don't want sour-dough. I like the other kind." She hung up.

McBride looked out at the slowly darkening sky. Lights were beginning to come on all around the bay; over in Oakland and Alameda across the Bay Bridge; over in Sausalito across the Golden Gate. Out in the middle, Alcatraz Island was a sour note, as gloomy and forbidding as ever. The rest of it was pretty beautiful, and McBride was a little regretful for some of the unpleasant things he'd said about San Francisco. He began laying out his dinner jacket and things that went with it. Between his teeth he whistled a few bars of *Make Believe*. He thought *Make Believe* was a swell song. When the knock on his door came he was brushing his teeth vigorously. He was as proud of his teeth as Sean O'Hara was of his small feet. Barefooted, in nothing but a pair of shorts he went to the door.

His visitor was Cyrus H.Q. Chandler. He stared a little uncertainly at McBride's dishabille. "May I come in, just for a moment?"

"Sure, why not?" McBride stood aside. Out in the hall a passing couple were properly shocked. McBride resisted the impulse to thumb his nose at them. He felt that one did not thumb one's nose in the presence of men like Cyrus H.Q. Chandler; not while pretending to be an equal, indeed a superior. No, the slightly arrogant touch was the thing. "Don't bother to thank me for giving—for rescuing Celeste this afternoon." He had almost said for giving her a leg up, but he wasn't going to be that horsily British for anybody. "It was nothing—nothing at all."

Chandler cleared his throat. In spite of his business background he was marked with the indelible aura of the Senate Investigating Committee; he was a sort of composite of Wendell Willkie and Martin Dies. He was the kind of man whom McBride thought ought to be coordinating a shuffleboard tournament instead of Pacific Coast war industries.

He said, "Well, as a matter of fact, my daughter seems rather—er vague about the whole thing. I thought that possibly you might-ah-clarify the situation for us."

McBride shook his head. His manner said that he must remain a gentleman at all costs. "Sorry, she was almost home when I first saw her." He watched the older man's face to see whether this statement gibed with any that Celeste herself might have made. As far as he could tell he had not stuck his neck out. "She didn't seem to want to talk about it, so I didn't press her."

"I appreciate your delicacy," Chandler said. His gesture was diffident, almost apologetic, but for a moment his eyes were as bright and keen as McBride's own. "Delilah—my wife—thought you mentioned something about an accident."

McBride shrugged. "Self-evident, wasn't it? People don't go around getting cuts on their wrists and runs in their stockings on purpose, do they?" He spread his hands. "It's none of my business, Mr. Chandler, but offhand I'd say maybe she'd had a drink or two too many, and was driving a car a bit too fast."

"Whose car?" Chandler's voice was suddenly a little rough around the edges.

McBride said gently, "Well, really, I'd hardly know that, would I?"

"No, I suppose not." Chandler turned as if to go out but paused to say, "I wouldn't have you think I'm spying on my daughter, Mr. McBride. I trust her implicitly." He sighed. "But at times she can be very stubborn."

McBride nodded an acknowledgment. "The younger generation," he said from the lofty heights of his own thirty-two years.

"I was afraid she might have hurt someone else, you see."

"Oh, I'm sure she didn't," McBride said. "If she had we'd have heard of it by this time."

"Of course," Mr. Chandler said. This time he actually got the door open. "You'll be staying on in San Francisco?"

"I can't help myself," McBride said. "The cops insist on it." He carefully explained about the death of one Severn alias Seversky, or vice versa. He could not see that the recital affected his guest one way or the other.

"No word about the Adelphi, then?"

"No."

"Delilah—my wife, you know—misses it," Chandler said. He became brisk. "Well, thank you again for your kindness to Celeste." An apparently sincere smile touched his rather full lips. "I'm even disposed to forgive you for suspecting us all. Good-night, Mr. McBride." He went away.

The telephone rang. Answering it against his better judgment McBride found himself listening to the suave voice of Mr. Sigmund Loeb. "Have you reached a decision yet, Mr. McBride?"

"About what?"

Loeb's voice descended to a throaty purr. "Shall we say about the item we discussed earlier today? I am a patient man, sir, but on the other hand, as a citizen, of course, I have certain obligations to the law." He sighed heavily. "You still do not wish to sell?"

McBride was furious. "I haven't got it, I tell you!"

"That is possible," Loeb said. "Perhaps a friend has it, eh?"

"I haven't any friends either!" McBride shouted. He became slightly reckless. "Go on and call copper and see if I care. You can't show that big nose of yours in it, and an anonymous phone call won't get you anything. The Hall's switchboard is full of them every day."

"Now you're just being silly," Loeb said calmly. "The Hall would like very much to have anything at all, even as flimsy a peg as a telephone call to hang Seversky's murder on.

And you with it, my impetuous young friend." He waited patiently till McBride ran out of invective. Then: "I had a telephone call myself a little while ago. A man seemed to think I would be interested in buying the item we both know about. Hence my remark about a possible friend."

McBride asked a rather inane question. "Who was it?"

"If I knew that would I be talking to you, Mr. McBride?" Loeb made sibilant, disparaging sounds with his lips. "I thought it somewhat an obvious trick of one wishing to remain anonymous. You, for instance."

McBride exercised admirable restraint. "Meaning I'd hire a go-between? Meaning I don't trust you, Siggy, old pal, old pal?"

"Well, sir, that is a moot question. Do you?"

"I do," McBride said earnestly. "I do and from now on I will." He looked out the window. "From where you're sitting can you see the Russ Building?"

"No."

"But you're familiar with it?"

"Certainly."

"Then all you've got to do," McBride said, "is imagine how far I could throw it with one hand. That's how far I trust you."

9

REPLETE WITH STEAK and French fries and salad and rolls and butter, and some very excellent ale furnished McBride by the same delicatessen which had furnished him the rolls, he leaned back in the angle made by chintz-covered windows and the breakfast-nook seat and admired his hostess. "Susan," he said earnestly, "you are a grand cook. Are you that good an accountant?"

Susan's face was still a little flushed from slaving all day over a hot stove, or at least for an hour. She had on a short-sleeved green-and-white checked print with a frilly white collar and there was a pleasant air of domesticity about being here like this with her. A vagrant wisp of copper-brown hair curled damply against her forehead and there were three freckles on her nose.

She said ruefully that she didn't think she was ever going to be a good accountant. "Not good enough to pass the State Board for CPA's."

He was fascinated by the golden glints in her brown eyes, and by her mouth which he had not yet kissed but thought he might before the evening was over. From where he sat he could see into the living-room, also bright with chintz but in a very expensive sort of way. There was a slow fire in the low fireplace under a tall blue-tinted mirror and the view through modernistic windows was the kind that goes with terrific rentals. He wondered a little how she could do it on a bookkeeper's salary, just as he had wondered about the Labrador mink coat of last night and the pair of silver foxes this noon.

"I must be in the wrong racket," he observed presently. "Either that or you've got a private income."

She read his thoughts. "Oh, that!" She giggled. "My salary is thirty-two fifty a week, but if I am a very good girl I am promised thirty-five by the end of the year."

"You'll never make it," McBride said.

"Why?"

"Because at thirty-two fifty a week this apartment says you are not a very good girl." He smiled across at her. "In fact it says you must be a very bad girl. Not," he added magnanimously, "that I have anything against bad girls." He brooded on that for a moment, remembering a certain girl he had known whom he had thought very good but who had turned out very bad; so bad indeed that he had had to send her up to the gas chamber. It had taken him three years, but he had almost forgotten her. "Bad girls and I seem to have an affinity." He told her a little about Celeste Chandler; not all of it.

Susan's color had deepened as he talked. "If I am as bad as you seem to think, there is no economic necessity for it. My people have some money, enough." She stood up and began removing some of the dishes. "You must visit us at Palo Alto some time."

He had the grace to flush. "All right, all right; I was just asking, wasn't I?"

She nodded. "I suppose it's like that, being a detective. You've got to know everything about everybody, each and every bracketed in his or her own little pair of parentheses." She went to the sink and from there she said, not turning, "You wouldn't happen to be jealous, would you?"

He shook his head. "You just remind me of someone, is all."

"Someone you knew very well?"

"Yes." He told her about that, too. He did not tell her about Kay Ford, for he saw no point in it. He discovered that she was regarding him with a kind of horror. "I know, you think it was a lousy thing to do. You probably think that if a man loves a woman he couldn't turn her up." His eyes were black with the memory of it. "Well, I did."

She thought that over for the space of two more trips to the sink. "Perhaps, if there were a point of honor involved—"

"Honor!" He sneered at the word. After a while he said, absently, "Pride maybe, I don't know." He began looking in the drawers of the sink cabinet for clean towels. "This little McGillicuddy-he in love with you?"

"Arthur?"

McBride laughed at her. "Don't tell me you know more than one McGillicuddy!"

Susan's nose wrinkled as she analyzed Arthur McGillicuddy's feeling for her. "Yes, I suppose he really is." She nodded decisively, but as though there were nothing personal in it; as though she were holding herself—and Arthur—off at arm's length and looking at them. "Yes." She ran scalding hot water over some plates. "Why?"

"I just wondered," McBride said.

"Something to do with that business at the Trojan?"

"Maybe."

Susan stamped her foot. "I just hate men who try to be enigmatic!"

Again McBride laughed. Unaccountably he found himself almost happy. Well, not happy, perhaps, but invigorated. He did not think it could be the ale, for he had only drunk three bottles. "Men are bastards," he said, and Susan agreed that this was so, and neither said anything more till after the dishes were put away and they had gone into the living-room.

A sudden restlessness seemed to have seized both of them, and the camaraderie of the kitchen was gone. She watched him moving about the room, picking up his discarded dinner jacket, laying it down again without putting it on; opening a book, but not really looking at it. She said, "Well, if we're going out I suppose I'd better get dressed," and he said, "Yes," and found a lone cigarette in a crumpled package, lit it and tossed the empty package into the fire.

At the bedroom door she paused and came back and stood before him. "What's the matter with us?"

"I forgot to ask how you felt about McGillicuddy," he said. "We only got as far as how he feels about you." His eyes narrowed against the smoke curling upward from the cigarette in his mouth. "Funny thing about that-I kind of like the little guy."

Susan's eyes laughed at him. "I thought honor wasn't in your lexicon."

"It isn't," McBride insisted. "I just like to feel that if I beat a guy's time he's my—"

"Your equal?"

"Well, yes."

"And Arthur isn't?"

"No."

"I like that," Susan said. "It's so—so self-sufficient. There goes a man, one says to one's self, who knows his own worth." She magically seemed to have grown taller, and the green-and-white checked print was become a languorous gown full of seduction. She took the cigarette from between his fingers, inhaled deeply from it and tossed it into the fire. "I'll watch Arthur's best interests, darling-and mine." She came into his arms. "You take care of yourself."

After a time she pushed him away. "Susan had really better get dressed now." She was breathing a little unevenly. "I'd no idea they kissed that way in the tropics."

"That's only the semi-tropics," McBride said modestly. "And even that's slightly diluted with San Francisco fog." He watched her into the bedroom and they carried on a desultory conversation through the partially open door.

She had, it appeared, queried Arthur McGillicuddy at some length during lunch regarding the general caliber of the Hotel Trojan's guests. McGillicuddy still insisted that he had never seen the very tall, very thin man described by McBride. He admitted that many of those who came and went had the furtive air of people on the wrong side of the law, but what would you? The Trojan was not exactly the type of hostelry which could be choosey. Ernest "Slugs" Foley may or may not have been married to the woman he called Marge. It was hardly the Trojan's place to demand sight of a marriage certificate, was it?

McBride said, "McGillicuddy ever see Foley and this Seversky together? Or Seversky and Marge?"

"No, I asked him that," Susan said. Her voice was slightly

muffled, as though she might have hairpins in her mouth. "They were all on the same floor, though, and even if they weren't, there was nothing to stop them exchanging visits."

"You're telling me," McBride said, remembering that Seversky had even exchanged rooms; his own for McBride's, and not only that, he had used McBride's room to get killed in. Some faint recollection of the exact circumstances recalled a thought. Seversky's window had been open; so had McBride's, directly beneath it. Suppose that Seversky had not actually met death in McBride's room after all? Suppose he had been killed upstairs and later carried down, possibly by way of the fire escape. At the thought McBride's scowl became a horrific thing. As an accident it was bad enough, but if the corpse had been planted on him with deliberate intent he was going to have to really do something about it.

Susan said, "What are you cursing about now?"

"I can't find any cigarettes," McBride said. He couldn't, either. Half a dozen very decorative but useless boxes scattered about the living-room contained nothing but crumbs, and he had used up the last of his own. He said indignantly, "A fine hostess, you are!"

"Well, you could run out and get some."

McBride sighed. "First it was the ale, then it was French rolls, now it's cigarettes." He put on his coat. "I don't know how McGillicuddy's going to support you in the style to which you're accustomed." He went out.

Emerging on the street a moment or two later, he discovered that one of the season's heavy fogs had sneaked up on him unawares. It was as thick as a hotel room after an all-night poker session. He could feel it cling to his skin; he could taste it, faintly salty and reminiscent of fish, on his lips. Street lamps, such as they were, had no more value as illumination than round yellow cheeses floating in skimmed milk. He decided he didn't want cigarettes bad enough to search for them without a guide, and was on the point of turning back into the lobby when a breeze lifted a corner of the fleecy blanket and he saw a car parked at the curb. It was a phaeton without side curtains and there was a woman at the wheel.

McBride crossed the sidewalk. "You wouldn't happen to have a spare cigarette, would you?"

"Sure." The woman turned her face toward him and he saw that she was Marge, the full-breasted blonde of the Hotel Trojan. From her lap she produced not a cigarette but a gun. She pointed the gun at McBride's white shirt front. "Sure I would, honey."

At the same instant McBride became aware of a presence behind him. Slugs Foley's tight, sandpapery voice said, "This is it, sucker." It was a hundred-to-one shot that the thing he pressed against McBride's kidneys was not a banana. "Get in the car, sucker. In beside Marge."

"No," McBride said. If it hadn't been for Marge's gun he would have taken a chance on Foley's. He could not beat both of them, and he knew it, but he saw no reason to make it easier for them by going riding first. "If you want to shoot me you can do it right here."

"Oh, one of them stubborn guys!" Foley's gun did not leave McBride's back, but he must have expected an argument and come prepared. A fistful of brass knuckles or something just as potent hit McBride behind the left ear and he sagged heavily against the car.

When consciousness returned to him the car was in motion and he was sitting right where Foley had told him to sit, in the front seat beside Marge. The car was in second gear, climbing steeply, its headlights boring a hole in the fog just deep enough to swallow the car a length at a time. Reflected in the windshield a cigarette alternately glowed and faded behind McBride; that would be Slugs Foley in the back seat. Marge looked straight ahead, driving fast but not recklessly. Her right hand guided the car. Her left, with the gun in it, lay along her left thigh, away from McBride.

At the crest of the hill they passed a cable car, a sluggish luminous bug, panting with the effort of the climb. McBride thought they must still be on California Street, though there was a cable line on Powell too. A lot of little demons with sledge hammers were having themselves a time inside his skull.

"I always kind of liked Seversky," Slugs Foley observed. "Didn't you, Marge?"

"Yeah."

McBride said angrily, "Now listen, you two; if you think I did that you're crazy!"

"Who else?"

"The cops think it might be you."

"Because you told them," Foley said. A sudden gust of smoke from his cigarette bathed the back of McBride's neck. "That's something else I owe you, sucker." An emotionless stream of obscenities dribbled from his lips. "By God, if I'd known who you were I'd have let you have it the first time I laid eyes on you."

Marge's laughter was like broken glass under foot. "The

house dick, he said he was!" It was obvious that she was keyed up to hysterical pitch. "The house dick!"

"Shut up, Marge," Foley said, a long-suffering parent admonishing a child. He addressed McBride again, "What did you do with the stuff, copper?"

"What stuff?"

Foley said, "Ahhh, that again," in a tired, disgusted voice. He said, "You might as well make up your mind to it, McBride, you're going to talk if we have to break every bone you got, one at a time. Everything was nice and cozy till you came along." He snapped his cigarette out the side of the car. "Now look at us. Nine million cops ready to pick us off on sight. Yeah, and get a medal for it, on account of we're supposed to have stuck that shiv in Seversky."

"Yeah," Marge said bitterly, "and it ain't only the cops. What about Deke?"

"Shut up, Marge!"

"What's the difference?" Her high-pitched, broken-glass laugh joined the clack of the windshield wipers. "We can't let this guy go walking around afterward, can we?"

The tires bumped over some car tracks and the phaeton began another steep ascent into impenetrable fog. Wherever they were, it was certainly not a well-traveled boulevard. McBride licked his lips. "Maybe the Deacon knocked him off. I met him coming out of Seversky's room."

There was an interval of silence, as though Foley might be thinking that over. Finally he said, "Naah, Deke ain't the type."

"Anybody's the type," McBride said, "if there's enough in it."

"Deke wouldn't take the chance," Foley said. "He'd have

us looking for him from hell to breakfast. Same like he's probably looking for us," he added moodily. The motor shrilled wildly for a moment as they reached the top of the grade and Marge disengaged the clutch for a shift. "No, you're our best bet, sucker." His laugh had a mirthless, out-of-the-world quality, as though he might be higher than a kite. "Maybe we can even get him to sign a confession, eh, Marge?"

"Yeah."

The car was plunging downward now, into a little valley from which the fog was strangely absent. There was an intersection of car lines, and some lighted store fronts indicated the presence of solid citizenry. McBride thought, "Well, this is it. I can't argue with hop-heads." He thrust his rump against Marge, pinning her gun hand against the side of the car; his left foot kicked her right one off the brake pedal, and as he fell over sideways, away from her, his left hand flicked the car out of gear.

Foley's first shot almost took McBride's ear off. The windshield shattered and there was a lot of noise. For no reason at all, except that she was rattled, Marge fell on top of McBride. The hurtling car went into a crazy dance, skidded sideways, hit some obstruction and turned over. It turned over at least twice and the phaeton top was like a collapsed parachute, smothering all three of the passengers, before the car hit something that was really solid.

McBride found that somehow, he never did know how, he had gotten into the back seat and was holding Foley's gun wrist with both hands. The car seemed to have stopped permanently and right-side up; the top and its broken supports billowed about the wrestling bodies of the two men, impeding their action if not their determination. There was no sound at all from Marge.

When Foley's gun finally went off, McBride discovered with some surprise that he had actually been successful in turning it in upon the man himself. Foley subsided. He subsided so instantly and completely that McBride knew he was dead even without looking.

Outside, out beyond the smothering folds of canvas, there were shouts now, and somewhere in the near distance a siren keened. Closer at hand, seeping into McBride's consciousness, there was the smell of raw gasoline and a sparking sputter as if someone with a short-wave set were sending. McBride thought he had better get out of there before the car became a flaming funeral pyre for all three of its occupants. He fumbled around for a doorcatch that would open, found one and crawled out into fresh night air.

Arms encircled him and hauled him erect and the owner of the arms said, "You are hokay, hanh?" He had a stained rubber apron on that stank to high heaven of fish.

McBride pushed him away. "Yeah." He began clawing at the flattened tepee which was the car's top. A lot of people materialized from nowhere and helped him. They got Marge out first, apparently uninjured except for a bruise over one eye, and carried her over and laid her on the sidewalk. Little mumbled incoherencies came from between her lips and presently she sat up and wiped them away with the back of a hand. Her eyes had a dazed, uncertain look and she seemed not to recognize McBride. He went back to the car.

The guy with the fish-saturated apron and two others had gotten Slugs Foley out and had just discovered that

Slugs had been shot. "Hah, theesa guy, she's been shot, no?" He stared with rising suspicion at McBride.

Three or four onlookers began closing in. "She did it," McBride said. He turned and pointed at the spot where they had left Marge. Marge wasn't there any more. She had vanished as completely and utterly as though she had never been.

It was at this instant that the sparking wire finally caught up with the spilled gasoline. There was a blinding gust of flame and everybody ran like hell. The wailing siren was very close now. It occurred to McBride that it would be most embarrassing to be caught in proximity to another dead man. He continued to run long after the others had stopped.

When he came into the apartment an hour or so later Susan was fully dressed and very indignant. "Where have you been?"

"Cigarettes," McBride said. A trifle self-consciously he laid a carton of Chesterfields on the table.

"All this time?" Susan demanded incredulously. "You've been gone over an hour!"

"They're hard to get," McBride said. In the blue-tinted mirror over the fireplace he saw that in spite of all his efforts he still looked slightly rumpled. The lump behind his left ear felt as big as his fist. "Priorities."

Susan saw the lump. There must have been a streak of sadism in her for she came up behind him and poked it viciously. "I see. You had to argue the man out of them."

"He thought I was a hold-up," McBride explained. He looked at some scratches in the palm of his hand. Glass from the windshield must have done that, he thought. "I had a hell of a time convincing him."

10

AROUND THE CRAP table the faces of the players seemed suspended in mid-air, curiously alike in their woodenness of expression, only the eyes alive and shifting with the galloping dice. The man with the dice was trying for an impossible five. He was working hard. Sweat stood out in oily yellow globules on his forehead, and though it was not hot in the great room, the palms of his hands were so moist he couldn't get a sound out of his snapping fingers.

Except for the stick man, calling the points in a flat disinterested voice and corralling the dice in the crook of his cane as they fell back off the baffle-boards, there was very little talking. On the far side of the table, the lookout and the two payoff men, assured of their regular dollar an hour no matter who else lost, were discussing the alleged rubber shortage. They were disembodied spirits too, only their eyes did not follow the dice. Their chief interest lay in their next fifteen-minute relief period.

McBride had a hundred dollars on the five. Under the brilliant white light his face was smooth and dark and unworried, though his hunch that this was his lucky night had not worked out so well. He was conscious of Susan at his elbow and a little behind him; a faintly disapproving Susan, though slightly excited too. Susan had won seventeen dollars at one of the roulette wheels and had quit, ignoring the importunities of the house shill to continue playing.

The little guy with the dice sevened out. The stick man said, "Up jumped the devil," and McBride, remembering the favorite line of a man he knew named George Landy, smiled at the little man and said, "Well, we get A for effort, anyway."

He turned away and saw Sean O'Hara looking at him from an open door across the gambling room. He nodded, but did not go over. Instead, he took Susan's arm and piloted her through the crowd to the small bar built across an alcove which probably had once been a bedroom. In spite of the carpeting and the press of people, the place had none of the opulent air of some that O'Hara had operated down South. It was like a barn. Overhead the bare rafters showed, and though the walls had been done over there was still evidence of where partitions had been knocked out. Faintly, from below, came the music of the Negro band in the supper room, muted not only by distance but by the hectic undertone of voices around the gambling tables.

McBride estimated the crowd at something less than two hundred, all pretty well-dressed and prosperous-looking. He thought that O'Hara must be doing all right. Susan sipped her rum Collins and watched people's faces. All the way out from the city, driving McBride in her small coupé, she had been strangely silent and he knew she was wondering what had happened to him but would not ask. As a matter of fact he could not put a finger on his reason for not telling her.

She had on a plain black dinner gown that, like the rest of her clothes he had seen, looked too expensive to go with a thirty-two fifty salary. There were coppery glints in her brown hair, reminding him of that other woman. He thought that probably it was because she was so like that other, and because he had been fooled once, that he watched his words with her, though he rarely talked to anyone about the case he was on, except maybe to lie.

He wondered if the police had yet identified Slugs Foley. He wondered too, a little, about Marge, and about Celeste Chandler, and Sean O'Hara, who was still watching him from that door at the far side of the room. Though the door was scarcely wider than O'Hara himself, McBride had the impression that the room behind him was some sort of office. He wondered how O'Hara had gotten there. The guard on the stairway leading up from below had said that O'Hara was not in, and certainly O'Hara had not come up those stairs since. McBride turned to the bartender and ordered another straight seltzer, pretending to Susan that he was just being virtuous. As a matter of fact, he had a gaseous, overfull feeling in the pit of his stomach, probably the result of the garlic Susan had put on the steak, though it was possible that wrestling around in the car with Slugs Foley hadn't done him any good. Certainly, he thought, it hadn't done Slugs Foley any good. He was mildly regretful about Slugs, because dead men rarely tell you anything you want to know.

Susan said, pointing, "Isn't that Cesar Romero over there?"

McBride saw that it was indeed Sebastian. The South American was in white tie and tails, and though he had bought a stack of chips and was scattering them over the numbers on a roulette layout, he had not surrendered his hat, stick or topcoat. He was not interested in the outcome of the wheel, one way or the other. He had the air of one who had just dropped in for a moment, or was killing time while waiting for someone. If he was conscious of McBride he did not show it.

It was Sean O'Hara who finally made the first move. Catching McBride's eye he lifted a large white hand and beckoned. McBride looked at Susan. "Excuse me, pet?"

Without waiting to see whether she would or not he put his glass down on the bar and crossed the room. "Hello, Sean."

O'Hara nodded. "Come in." A faint smell of fog still clung to his clothes and there was a stain of some kind on the inside edge of his small left shoe, down near the sole. It was obvious that he had been out in the night and it was still a minor mystery, at least to McBride, how he had got back in without coming up the only stairs in sight.

The office itself offered no clue to the mystery. It was just an office, paneled shoulder high in burl walnut and rather opulently fitted up, but the only other door was wide open, disclosing a combination clothespress and lavatory. McBride had a brief moment in which he visualized eyes watching him from some secret recess behind the walnut panels; and concealed stairs and pale clawing hands reminiscent of the earlier Karloff horror pictures.

He decided that the whole business must be conjured up by the underlying note of menace in O'Hara's own manner. The fat man was not cordial. He was distinctly not cordial. He closed the door and leaned his broad back against it, eyeing McBride from beneath pouchy lids. "This your first trip out here?"

McBride appeared surprised. "Why, yes."

"You weren't out here, say, earlier in the day—this afternoon?"

"No."

O'Hara's dress shirt was slightly mussed. It rose and fell, once, over his massive bosom. "All right." His tapering, top-like body moved over behind the desk and creaked into a protesting chair. He pushed an open humidor across the desk. "Have a cigar, McBride."

McBride's eyes were bright and hard and a little angry. "Not until you tell me what this is all about."

"Forget it."

McBride's mouth was stubborn. "No."

O'Hara lifted a placating hand. "Don't go Irish on me, Rex. I lost something this afternoon and I thought you might have seen it happen, that's all." With careful nicety he clipped a cigar and rolled the end between his full lips. "Forget it."

McBride decided to be mollified. "Well, all right." He, too, helped himself to a cigar.

"Been thinking over my proposition?"

"Unh-hunh."

O'Hara took time out to get his cigar burning evenly. Rich, aromatic smoke climbed up around his great head and formed a kind of halo over the smoothly brushed white hair. "Well?"

McBride shook his head regretfully. "I can't leave Frisco yet, Scan. Maybe Monday or Tuesday, I don't know yet. Seversky's inquest is Monday." He watched O'Hara's face. "You get a line on this Slugs Foley for me?"

"Foley is dead."

McBride thought the grapevine must be working even faster than usual. His eyes mirrored a vast surprise. "The hell he is!"

"Yep," O'Hara said. He felt called upon to explain his knowledge. "One of the boys was down at the Hall when the word came in." He laughed without a great deal of humor. "Slugs lived up to his name until the very last. Somebody put one smack in his heart." Quite suddenly he lifted his eyes and put them, intent and steely, on McBride's face. "Bad for you—if people knew you were looking for him."

By "people" he meant the police. McBride shrugged that off. "The cops were looking for him, too."

"But the cops didn't shoot him," O'Hara said. He looked at a point behind and slightly to the left of McBride. "Well, Bogey?"

McBride had to use a deal of restraint to keep from whirling. When he did turn it was casually, without hurry. He saw that a man had come in from somewhere, probably from the main gambling room, though he had not heard the door open, nor did he know how long the man had been standing there watching him. The man was the gorilla of the graveled front yard; the one Butch had conked with a cobblestone. He nodded his ugly, misshapen head. "It was him," he said.

McBride's laugh was pure bravado, and he knew that O'Hara knew that it was. He said, "What does that mean?"

O'Hara did none of the usual things. He did not produce a gun and point it at McBride; he did not curse, nor hurl his chair back, nor say he knew it all the time. He just sat there quietly and considered McBride as he would the back of the hole card in a stud game. Presently he said, "You know what it means, Rex. I don't have to tell you."

The man Bogey made animal sounds deep down in his throat; sounds McBride construed as indicating pleasurable anticipation of what was to come. McBride wondered if the cobblestone was responsible for Bogey's lopsided face. He could not remember how Bogey's face had looked before.

Silence settled on the room; a silence pregnant with meaning to one familiar with the stories about Sean O'Hara. McBride licked his lips. "I never saw this guy before in my life."

O'Hara was politely unimpressed by the denial. "Even without Bogey's identification I had enough to give me ideas, McBride. You were working on the Adelphi necklace. You thought Celeste Chandler might have copped it. You found Celeste Chandler this afternoon—here." He sighed. "I don't like people interfering in my business, McBride."

There was a thunderous rapping on the door. And then, without waiting for an invitation which he probably knew wouldn't come anyway, the knocker opened the door. He was Lieutenant Nick Orsatti and he had two other cops with him. All three had their guns out and all three pointed them smack at McBride. Orsatti was jubilant. He appealed to his little helpers. "Didn't I tell you? If you don't find a guy one place you always find him some place else." He pushed the derby to the back of his head, exposing flattened, oily ringlets of black hair. Somewhere in the excitement he had managed to lose his toothpick, but otherwise he looked about the same. Under the ceiling lights there was a positive halation from his shiny blue serge. "They want to talk to you down at the Hall, McBride."

O'Hara said in a tight, bleak voice, "Get out, copper. You're off your beat out here."

"There's some Sheriff's men downstairs," Orsatti said. He grinned toothily. "Want me to prove it?" His fat, sly eyes encompassed the room. "You're getting along all right out here, Mr. O'Hara. You wouldn't want to ruin it all to protect a client, would you?"

McBride's breath came back in a rush. He detested Orsatti. He hated him. He had never been so glad to see anybody in his life. "O'Hara doesn't have to protect me, copper. I'll be glad to go with you." He took a cagey step toward the door, holding his wrists out as though for the cuffs. "Who am I supposed to have killed this time?"

Orsatti's wink included O'Hara, the gorilla Bogey and his own two men. "Did I say he killed anybody?" He leered. "No sir, I didn't." He positively beamed on McBride. "You hear about Celeste Chandler having an accident this afternoon?"

With the Marines to the rescue McBride saw no harm in admitting that now. "Why, yes," he said. He looked at O'Hara. "I picked her up wandering around half dazed outside the hotel."

"Well, sir," Orsatti said happily, "that broad just can't seem to stay away from accidents. She had another one tonight." His belly shook at the memory. "This one was fatal."

11

SHE LAY ON one of the high white mobile tables in the autopsy surgeon's room, though the surgeon had long since finished and they had put her clothes back on her small crushed body. The clothes themselves had suffered considerably, and clearly apparent in the wool fabric of her skirt and coat there were the marks of muddy automobile tires. Under the cruel white light she looked like a brutalized child, and McBride had the curious thought that she could not have fared much worse if she had been left in Belgium when the Nazis came. A police photographer, obviously not for the first time, was making some exposures of her right hand. In an anteroom a woman's sobs cut through the stillness—Delilah Chandler's, and her husband's voice came hushed and repressed, trying to quiet her.

In the surgery McBride watched the photographer. Orsatti and the red-haired Captain Wick and the assistant prosecutor who looked a little like Arthur McGillicuddy watched McBride. The scene was calculated to make McBride break down and confess, for the hand the photographer was working on refuted the evidence of the tire marks on the clothes, and the broken bones and contusions beneath them. Not that anyone doubted the existence of an automobile. Celeste had been hit by one, and run over by one, possibly more than once, but the hand said that it was not an accident. A thumb and two of the fingers had been individually seized and crushed, as between the jaws of a nutcracker or a pair of pliers. The killer had been a little careless there, McBride thought. He controlled an impulse to go somewhere and be sick at his stomach.

Orsatti said, "You killed her. You've been chasing hell out of her and something happened, so you killed her."

"Sure," McBride said. "I tried it this afternoon, only it didn't take, so I let her go back home to rest up for another attempt." Angry color came into his face and he pointed a shaking finger at Captain Wick's nose. "Listen, I'm getting goddam sick of being dragged down here whenever Orsatti happens to feel like it. Keep him off me or I'm going to take him apart."

"Orsatti's got a job to do," Wick said. After a while he said thoughtfully, "So have I." A freckled forefinger poked at his bristly red mustache. "Funny thing, that accident she had this afternoon." He stared intently at McBride's chin. "Maybe it really was an accident. Maybe that's what gave you the idea for another one."

"Me and nineteen other guys," McBride said.

"Maybe," Wick nodded. He searched his pockets for a cigar, finally found one that was almost as badly mangled as Celeste Chandler, licked it into shape and put it a little absently back in his pocket. "The trouble is, we don't know about the nineteen other guys. We do know about you."

"All right," McBride said, "tell me why I did it."

Wick appeared surprised. "Why, didn't you know?" He fiddled with the heavy gold watch chain looped across his vest. "She stole—or arranged to have stolen—the Adelphi necklace. You told us that yourself." He sighed. "You couldn't prove it without turning the heat on her, so you turned it on and it backfired. She died on you."

McBride sneered. "But not before she told me where it was, I'll bet!"

"We wouldn't know about that," Wick said. "We'll find out."

McBride looked at the assistant prosecutor. "You're probably as biased as the cops but you ought to be a little more intelligent. What am I supposed to do with this necklace when I get it? Or even say I've already got it… I can't very well just turn it back to my company without explaining the circumstances under which it was recovered."

"I'm afraid it's a little past the time for ordinary explanations," the prosecutor agreed. "Seversky's murder, and now this one, prohibit the kind of deal we talked about this morning." He shook his head. "The thing is still very valuable, even broken up and fenced." The rimless lenses of his pince-nez glinted in the strong light. "Money is not so easily traceable as a diamond necklace, Mr. McBride. It occurs to me that—"

"So now I'm going to fence it for salvage and turn the money over to my company!"

Orsatti cursed. "Nuts, what's all this talk about? Let's throw him in the can and call it a day. I'm tired."

McBride looked at him. "Keep on, Wop."

Captain Wick said heavily, "Well, let's go upstairs."

Out in the corridor a couple of harness bulls ranged themselves on either side of McBride and they all went up to Wick's office. Two other cops were entertaining, or being entertained by, Susan Lee. They seemed to be having a pretty good time. McBride looked at her. "Who let you in?"

"Oh, I just sort of trailed along," Susan said. "At a careful distance, of course." She stared at Orsatti. "I didn't want to get contaminated."

Wick said, "Now see here, Miss—uh—Miss—"

"Lee," Susan supplied. She smiled at the assistant prosecutor. "Some reporters told me that Miss Chandler died at approximately nine o'clock." Her lifted eyebrows suggested that if her information was incorrect now was the time for him to say so. When he did not she turned her radiant smile on Captain Wick. "Well, then, whatever McBride is accused of, he couldn't have done—he simply couldn't have, because, you see, he was with me from a little after seven until the officers came for him."

For a moment Wick and the prosecutor were struck speechless. Not so Orsatti. "She's lying!" he yelled, and took a swift step towards her. "You lying little tramp!"

McBride interposed his own bulk between them. He hit Orsatti in the mouth, hard, and felt Orsatti's teeth give under the impact and watched him fall. "I owe you that one on two counts," he said carefully. "Once for smacking me, and once for not being a gentleman." He permitted the two harness bulls to wrestle him back to his former position. He looked at Wick with insolent eyes. "You can't even stick me for that. I was protecting a lady from assault."

Orsatti got raging to his feet. "You son of a bitch!"

McBride appealed to the assistant prosecutor. "You see?"

Wick was furious and doing his best not to show it. He pointed an accusing finger at Susan. "Young lady, are you ready to swear to the statement you just made?"

"Of course."

"You know the penalty for perjury?"

"No," Susan said calmly, "but I'm sure it must be something horrible." She addressed herself to the prosecutor, whom she seemed to like. "Mr. McBride dined with me at my apartment. From there we went out to Burlingame."

"And he was never out of your sight for a moment?"

Susan blushed prettily. "Well, perhaps for a moment. After all—" Her embarrassment made heels out of all of them for asking too intimate questions.

The prosecutor looked slightly flustered. "Sorry, Miss Lee, but modesty has no place in a murder investigation." He consulted a slip of paper thrust at him by Captain Wick. He made some mental calculations, probably as to distances. Indeed his next question verified this assumption. "You are prepared to swear that he was not out of your sight or hearing for more than fifteen minutes during all that time?"

"Oh my goodness, yes," Susan said. "Why, I even left my door partially open while I was changing." She thought a moment. "Of course I couldn't actually see or hear him when he was in with Mr. O'Hara, but that was much later, wasn't it?"

The prosecutor agreed that that had been much later. He seemed relieved rather than otherwise. He looked from Orsatti to Captain Wick. "Well, that rather takes care of the Foley job too, doesn't it?"

Orsatti quit sucking at a loosened tooth. "Unless she's lying. Which she is."

McBride said quickly, "What's this about Foley?" He

was amazed that they hadn't rounded up the half-dozen witnesses who could identify him.

"As if you didn't know!"

"All right," McBride said, "the hell with you! I'll read it in the papers." He looked at Wick. "Anything else you want to horse me around about?"

"No," Wick said. His pale hard eyes rested on Susan's face. "For your sake, young lady, I hope you're telling the truth." He appeared to think that over. "Still, if for any reason you decide to—ah—reconsider your story, you may come to me and I think I can promise you—"

Orsatti said through twisted puffy lips, "Give me ten minutes alone with her and she'll reconsider it."

Susan examined him with the calm scrutiny of a scientist. "I must remember never to be alone with you," she said. She accepted McBride's arm and they went out. All the way to the street they could hear Orsatti cursing. Susan said, very low, "He isn't through, is he? They didn't really believe me."

"No," McBride said. "They'll keep coming back until they sew me up tighter than a strait-jacket—or until I break the case for them." He put an arm around her. "Just the same, you were swell, beautiful! You got me a reprieve."

She pushed him away. "I'd rather you didn't touch me just now, Rex. Not for a little while." Her voice had a tight, strained sound. "Not until I—"

He stared down at her. A strong wind had thinned the fog almost to the vanishing point and he could see her face quite plainly. "Well, for Christ's sake, you think I did it!"

"Don't bother to lie to me, too," she said tiredly. "You

were gone for over an hour." She opened the door of her car. "Good-night, Rex."

He seized her arm. "Listen, if you feel that way about it why did you come up with an alibi?"

She shook her head, as though her reasons were not very clear in her own mind. "I don't know."

"Get in the car," he said roughly. "There are a couple of things we've got to get straightened out right now." He climbed in after her and banged the door shut. Not looking at him, staring fixedly through the windshield, she began to drive, cutting across towards the Presidio and the Golden Gate bridge. A string of half a dozen wildly tooting cars went by them. On the last one was a crudely lettered canvas sign which said: "Just Married."

McBride began to talk in a low matter-of-fact voice. "I'm no good, Susan, and if you've got any ideas like the one on that sign just ahead you might as well get over them right now." He thought of something. "Or if you've been reading some of our more lurid literature about gun molls and one thing and another." He drew a slow breath. "But for your information, I don't go around knocking off gals and making it look like an accident." He told her about the Slugs Foley and Marge incident. "That's where I was during the hour you and the cops are worried about."

Still she would not look at him. "Why didn't you tell them that?"

"I might have," he said sourly, "if you hadn't stuck your neck out with an alibi." And then when he saw her flinch: "Forget it, I probably wouldn't have told them a goddam thing." He blew on the set of knuckles Orsatti's teeth had skinned and rubbed them in the palm of his other hand.

"Matter of fact, if Orsatti knew I was within a mile of the Foleys he'd swear it was I who kidnaped them." He touched her knee and said more gently, "That's something we'll have to look out for, hon. Half a dozen guys helped me haul Marge and Foley out of that car. They were pretty excited, but just the same, if Orsatti holds me up in front of them he's liable to get a positive identification." His eyes brooded over the possibility. "If he does that, your story is shot full of holes and it won't be very pleasant for you." After a while he said, "Nor for me, either. In that hour or so I probably had time to knock off Slugs and Celeste Chandler, too."

Susan began to laugh a trifle hysterically. "That last sentence almost puts us right back where we started, doesn't it?" She accelerated the speed of the car as they swung off Presidio Drive and began to make a sort of grand circle of Golden Gate Park. Presently she said, "I do believe you, though." And still later: "But if you didn't do it, who did?"

"I don't know," McBride said. He did not tell her about Sean O'Hara.

12

SOME SIXTH SENSE warned McBride that he had company even before he fitted his room key into the lock. It was very quiet there in the corridor, and dim, as it should be at one o'clock in the morning, but McBride was still mindful of what he had found on opening a door in the Hotel Trojan. His sixth sense told him that there was no reason to expect anything more pleasant on the far side of this door in the Hotel St. Mark. Apparently everybody in San Francisco was bent on making life not only hard but uncertain for a man named McBride. He stood there, holding the key with its heavy metal tag muffled in his hand so that it wouldn't rattle and precipitate a burst of shell fire from the other side of the door.

Unfortunately-or perhaps fortunately-his two guns were in there somewhere with the intruder. If he had had even one of them he might have been tempted to open the door and engage in a duel; a somewhat one-sided duel at best, for this short length of hall ended in the door and he would have had a whole room in which to look for his target, whereas the other guy only had to concentrate on the door and the hall behind it. McBride felt that even a very lousy shot indeed could not miss under those circumstances. He retreated carefully to the main corridor and backed along that, keeping his eyes on the mouth of his own short hall, until he came to the elevators. He punched all of the down buttons, one after the other.

Two cars arrived almost simultaneously. "Would you mind having the house dick come up?" McBride said. "There's someone in my room."

The operators were Chinese girls in brocaded silk pajamas. One of them asked the obvious question: "How do you know?"

"I'm psychic," McBride said. Mentally he chose the taller of the two, the one who said nothing at all. He wondered how a Chinese girl would be. He said, "You can stay here and protect me if you like. It won't take both of you to find the house dick."

The girl who always had to ask questions first, slammed the car door and the bronze indicator above them unwound from 12 to 1. The tall girl continued to look gravely at McBride. She was really very good-looking. She had had a permanent wave and her skin was the color of tree-ripened apricots. The yellow silk mandarin coat clung to her small firm breasts. Her finger-nails were scarlet. She said, "Are you sure you know what you're doing?"

McBride stared at her in some surprise. "I think so."

"It might be Mrs. Chandler," the girl said.

McBride was intrigued. "Might it, lovely? Whatever gave you that idea?"

"Earlier this evening she wanted to know if I had a pass-key."

"No!"

"Yes."

McBride smiled at her. "And what did you tell her, pet?"

"That I hadn't one." The girl did not smile back. McBride

thought that he would probably grow tired of her after a while. Though they were a different color her eyes had the same uncomfortably penetrant quality as Miss Ford's. She said, "She may have gotten one from someone else."

"There's always that," McBride agreed. His eyes grew bright and hard and a little cruel. "Personally, I hope it isn't Mrs. Chandler. I like to carry my ladies over the threshold."

The other car came up with a rush, and a spare, competent-looking man who said he was the house dick got out. He dismissed the two girls with a nod. He took a gun from beneath his left armpit and held it carelessly down at his side. "Let's see what we've got here."

McBride said, "It's only fair to warn you that a lot of people don't like me in this town. Whoever's in there won't be a common sneak thief."

The houseman was not the usual hotel bull who wants to show off. He considered McBride's information carefully; he considered the branch corridor leading to McBride's suite and another running parallel to it, leading to a window with a shaded red globe over it. "Tell you what we could do," he said. "One of us could take the fire escape and maybe get at one of your windows that way. If a guy made enough noise it might scare our party out into the hall."

McBride couldn't think of a better plan. He magnanimously allowed the house dick to risk his neck on the narrow stone ledge beyond the fire-escape landing. He himself took up a position flat against the wall of the main corridor and hidden from view of party or parties unknown who might emerge from his door. He could hear the houseman bang the window up; hear feet scrabbling on iron rungs and then sandpapering along stone. He was so busy listening to those things that he almost missed the scurry of movement on the thick carpeting of the hall. A man came very quickly out of the short lateral, turned toward the elevators, saw McBride, whirled in the opposite direction with a choked cry and ran for the stairs. He was Mr. Cyrus H.Q. Chandler.

McBride caught him in three strides and a plunging tackle which brought them both to the floor with a terrific thump. Being on the bottom, and about thirty years older, it was Cyrus Chandler who lost the ensuing wrestling bout. During the struggle neither man had said anything; only their threshing bodies making noise. Along the hall, two or three doors came open and some people looked out.

"Be nice," McBride said in Chandler's ear. He hauled the panting, paunchy and very disheveled man to his feet just as the house dick came around the turn from the fire-escape ell. McBride did not release his prisoner but he held him as though just steadying a friend that had fallen. "Sorry to disturb you folks," he said evenly. "My pal is given to practical jokes and for a moment"—his nod linked the house dick with himself "—we thought we had something." He urged Chandler into the lateral passage and through his own door.

The house dick followed them in, closing the door gently and leaning his back against it. Obviously he was not going to be put off with so flimsy an explanation as McBride had accorded the other witnesses. Obviously too, he recognized Chandler and was not making any accusations except those he could prove. "Gun," he said, pointing to where one lay on the carpet in front of the divan. "He had it trained on the door you were supposed to come through."

McBride thrust Chandler deep into a club chair, not roughly but with a sort of finality. He went over and picked up the gun. It was one of his own. The butt plates were still moist, as though Chandler might have been sweating at the prospect of what he was about to do. McBride looked at the house dick. "Mine." He looked at the gray-faced Chandler. "I didn't kill her, you know. A lot of people think I did, but they're wrong." He put the gun in his pocket and sat on an arm of the divan, swinging one leg back and forth, back and forth, as though measuring off the ticking of a clock. His eyes were remote, without either anger or reproach. In the silence Chandler's breathing had the agonized sound of fingers screeching across a taut drumhead.

The house dick cleared his throat. "Well, I don't know about this—"

McBride shrugged. "I can forget it if you can." He made a gesture towards his pocket, looked at the man's face. "No, you're not the kind I'd offer money to."

Chandler suddenly buried his face in his hands. "For God's sake!" He began to sob, not noisily. McBride watched him for a moment, still with that curiously aloof expression in his eyes. Presently he said, speaking to the house dick and as though he had given the matter a great deal of thought, "His daughter's death has upset him. Some people are like that, I guess. They just have to go off the deep end,"

"I'll have to make a report," the houseman said stubbornly.

"Sure you will," McBride said.

"But if you don't swear out a complaint—"

McBride nodded pleasantly. "That's the general idea." He stood up and held out his hand. "Thanks."

"Thank you," the house dick said. "I—that is, the St. Mark—" He was embarrassed. "Well, the truth is, we don't often meet your kind, McBride. If there's ever anything we can do to show our appreciation—"

"There is," McBride said. "Tell the help on the desk downstairs that if any cops come around—especially a fat slob named Orsatti—they're to act like they never heard of me."

The houseman jerked a nod in Chandler's direction. "What about him?"

"I'll take care of him," McBride said. He shook his head slightly at the sudden look of comprehension on the man's face. "No, nothing like that, chum. I just want to talk to him for a while." He held the door open and said good-night and waited till he heard the elevator come up and go down again. Even after he had closed the door and locked it he did not immediately address the stricken man in the club chair. He went over to the console against the far wall and poured himself a slug of rye from the quart bottle on a tray, swishing the liquor around in his mouth as though trying to get rid of a bad taste. He found that without much trouble he could visualize a guy named Rex McBride lying out there in the hall with a bullet hole, maybe more than one, in his stomach. His belly muscles contracted, as though recoiling from the impact. He had another drink.

Chandler shuddered violently and uncovered his face. The flesh beneath his skin seemed to have shrunk; the skin sagged in loose, unhealthy folds, the color of Malaga grapes. "Could I—could you spare me a little of that?"

"Sure." McBride filled a water tumbler half full and carried it over. He was surprised that he felt so little animosity toward the man who had been about to kill him. He was a trifle smug in the knowledge that here was further proof, had he needed any, of the petty human frailties motivating the so-called big shots. This guy, a political appointee, was entrusted with state secrets, with a part in the most important job in the world at the moment, and here he was, acting on impulse, with no more thought of the consequences than a cheap hop-head hoodlum like Slugs Foley.

The liquor had helped Chandler a little. Some of the palsy had gone out of his hands and the skin around his jaws no longer quivered when he drew a breath. "I was— fond of Celeste," he said presently, "and when the police let you go I—well, I guess I sort of lost my head." He shivered. "There's no use saying I just intended to force a confession from you." He wiped the back of a hand across his eyes as though to clear his vision. "I—I don't know what I would have done."

"Forget it."

"No!" Chandler said sharply. After a while he lifted haggard eyes to McBride's face. "Why are you doing this for me?"

"Because it makes me bigger than you," McBride said with unaccustomed honesty. "I like the feel of it. But just so you won't get the idea that I'm a complete fool, don't give me that 'fond of Celeste' line. You were nuts about her, and not like a father either." He began moving about the living-room, not nervously but as though he thought better when his body was in motion. "Except for one or two things, I'd say you knocked her off yourself." He did not mention what the one or two things were. "You were crazy jealous of the way she was carrying on with Sebastian." He thought of something. "Maybe the torture angle was just a cover-up, meant to make the kill look like something else."

Chandler got to his feet with something approximating his normal dignity. "I am a married man, sir. What you insinuate is unthinkable." A sudden trembling came into his knees and he steadied himself against the back of the heavy chair. "I—I love my wife."

McBride thought cynically that, if true, the love Chandler vowed was not reciprocated. It occurred to him that he had even a better case against Delilah than he had against Chandler. He discovered that he was deliberately fighting shy of Sean O'Hara, against whom he had the best case of all. O'Hara had copped her off once. Celeste herself had admitted owing the gambler money. It seemed perfectly obvious that O'Hara had tried again, this time with a reasonable degree of success. Certainly the police would think so, if possessed of only part of McBride's knowledge. McBride could not have told you why he had withheld that knowledge; why he intended to go on withholding it, at least for a while. Perhaps it was because he had not yet found the key; the key which would unlock the door between him and the Adelphi necklace. He wanted the Adelphi like nobody's business, but now he wanted it only under certain circumstances. The mere possession of it, without somebody to take the rap for the Seversky kill, and Foley's, and now Celeste Chandler's, would be equivalent to a one-way ticket to the gas chamber.

Try as he would he could find no connection between

Celeste and Seversky; between Celeste and Slugs Foley and that shadowy figure hovering somewhere in the background, the Deacon. Nor was there any apparent connection between O'Hara and any of these save Celeste. It occurred to him, not for the first time, that the two killings he didn't know about—Seversky's and Celeste's—might be unrelated. One of them might have nothing whatever to do with the missing necklace. He stubbornly pushed the thought from him, because if Celeste, or Delilah—or Chandler himself—hadn't in some way engineered the original theft, then he, McBride, was a fool and could no longer have any faith in his hunches.

He became conscious of Cyrus Chandler replenishing his tumbler from the bottle of rye. "Where'd you get the key?"

"From a bellboy."

McBride recalled what the Chinese girl had told him. "Your wife help you?"

Chandler appeared genuinely surprised. "Certainly not. Why should you think that?"

"It was just an idea." For no reason at all McBride had another one. "Tell me about this Sebastian guy. Known him a long time?"

Chandler flushed. "See here, if you're obsessed with the jealousy theory—" After a while he said, almost sullenly, "We've known him for several years. Ever since I was a vice-consul to Para."

McBride thought the jealousy theory wasn't so terrifically silly. He thought Chandler himself should have subscribed to it on two counts—Celeste *and* Delilah. The only thing was, the wrong party seemed to have been killed.

It should have been Mr. Rodriguez Franz Sebastian. He said, "Well, you'd better give the key back to the bellhop. You might be tempted to use it again."

Chandler looked at him. "Mr. McBride, I've resented you. Certainly we've never been friends and after this— after tonight—I don't suppose we ever shall be." He drew a slow breath. "But if it was not you who murdered my daughter, and you can produce the man who did, you can name your own ticket." He straightened his shoulders and moved heavily towards the door.

"Good-night," McBride said. He was very careful to put the safety chain in place after his departing guest.

13

A LITTLE ASTONISHED at having enjoyed a good night's rest, and rather pleased with it, for it showed his conscience either callous or guiltless, McBride awoke to a nine o'clock Sunday morning filled with one of San Francisco's better grade fogs. The windows dripped with it. In Los Angeles or Baltimore or even Calcutta it would have been called rain, but not in San Francisco. This one was the color of the Venetian blinds and as far as McBride could see it had about the same substance. Even though the bedroom windows were closed and locked against a possible assailant equipped with an airplane or parachute, McBride could actually taste the stuff on his lips. It tasted salty, with just a dash of oakum. McBride reached out to the night-stand between the twin beds and got a cigarette alight. Then, covers pulled up to his chin, he gave himself over to the pure luxury of what good—or at least fictional—detectives are supposed to employ when in a quandary: ratiocination.

The hell with all this running around, he thought. The hell with wearing my shoes down to the last eyelet when I can just lie here and let the Induction-Deduction Twins do my work for me. Let's see, now, what was it Rourke hired me to do? Oh yes, to get the Adelphi necklace back! Well, hell, that's simple enough. All you've got to do is find the guy that's got it and take it away from him. All right, then; so far, so good. Now who do we think has got it?

It was at this point that Deduction and Induction deserted McBride completely. He cursed them impartially and reached for the telephone extension. "Get me the warden at San Quentin," he told the hotel operator who answered. "Tell him it's Captain Wick of the homicide detail." He cradled the phone and got up and padded out to the hall door in his bare feet. The management of the St. Mark apparently still regarded him as a guest worth cultivating. There was the advertised tray with the thermos of coffee and all the morning papers. Shivering, McBride retreated to the bed, pausing en route only long enough to turn all the radiators on full blast.

Both of the papers had given the war second billing. Celeste Chandler got first. There were columns of information about her rescue from Belgium, her adoption by the Chandlers and her subsequent activities under their tutelage. There was a picture of Delilah and one of Cyrus H.Q. as the bereaved parents; a list of his official and semi-official positions that read like a Cook's Tour; a carefully compiled family tree and social history for Delilah; a eulogy of Cyrus which led you to believe that though he was not exactly a dollar-a-year man, he had given up a great deal in order to serve his country in his present capacity of WPB coordinator for the Pacific Coast. There was not one single word about the three mangled fingers on Celeste's right hand. The police were looking for a hit-and-run driver.

McBride knew this was not so. His respect for San Francisco's police department increased accordingly. For once they were playing it smart.

On Page 2 there was a reasonably accurate account of the Slugs Foley affair. The police had not been able to disguise this as an accident, the reporters having arrived on the scene coincident with the cops themselves. It was even alleged that this was a continuation of the "gang war" which had begun with the murder of one Seversky in an unnamed hotel. Foley himself had been wanted by the police in connection with that kill, and it was believed that the "mystery woman" of the wrecked car was the same one who had been registered at the hotel as his wife.

The third occupant of the death car was described as a gentleman. "He was wearing a tuxedo," three witnesses had stated. McBride was relieved that the expanse of white shirt front had apparently blinded the witnesses to the face above it. A man who said he was in the wholesale fish business quoted the "gentleman" as saying, "She did it," while pointing at the "mystery woman."

A fire believed to be of incendiary origin had swept through an Oakland shipyard early this morning. The damage was estimated at half a million dollars. The FBI was investigating.

The funnies were not funny.

McBride was pouring a second cup of coffee when the telephone rang. The warden of San Quentin was away over the week-end, and would his deputy do? McBride said he would and presently was connected with a man who thought McBride was Captain Wick of Homicide and saw nothing unusual in Captain Wick calling from a suite in the St. Mark. "We seem to have mislaid the file on a con called the Deacon," McBride said. "You people released him either Thursday or Friday. What's his full name again?"

"Just a minute, I'll look it up."

Five minutes later McBride was in possession of some interesting if not too helpful information about Clyde Clement, alias the Deacon, alias Deke, etc., etc. It turned out that the Deacon had served two raps for forgery and a third—the last for embezzlement. The complainant was the Hollywood Park Racing Association. The Deacon had been an accountant there, and some of the money passing through his hands had stuck. So far as known he had no San Francisco addresses. He had been committed from Los Angeles.

"Visitors?" McBride said.

The deputy resorted to his records again. "Only one recently," he said. "A man named— Hey, wait a minute! Wasn't there a man named Seversky killed up there night before last?"

"Keep it under your hat," McBride said. "We don't want to push this out in the open yet." After a moment he said, "When was the last time Seversky visited him?"

"Two weeks ago. You don't think—?"

"No," McBride said sourly. "Hardly ever." He hung up.

Reviewing events and probabilities that were likely to become events he concluded that he ought to be hearing from Sean O'Hara pretty soon. The grapevine had tipped the gambler to Slugs Foley's death almost as soon as it happened; it was not inconceivable that the same grapevine would apprise him of the true facts about Celeste Chandler. Especially was this true in view of McBride's arrest. O'Hara would have every right to expect McBride to talk in order to clear himself. And if McBride talked about what O'Hara had done to Celeste earlier in the day, her subsequent death was bound to look pretty bad for Sean O'Hara. Ergo, O'Hara must assuredly take steps to see that if McBride had not already talked, he would not do so in the future. McBride decided that he would have to be even more watchful than usual from now on.

He picked up the phone once more and began calling the various newspapers. In each he inserted a personal: "Clyde, Marge needs you. Telephone CH 2437." The number was Susan Lee's. McBride expected little to come of this, but it was worth a try. The Deacon might also need Marge. McBride needed them both.

He rang Susan to tell her about the ads and found she was just departing for church. "Like to go with me?"

McBride shuddered violently. "No."

"Confession is good for the soul, darling."

"I haven't any soul," McBride said. "Besides, someone is knocking on the door." He hung up, because his last statement was truth in all its purity. Someone really was knocking.

On the way out he thoughtfully provided himself with a gun and approached the door cautiously and at an angle, so that anyone trying to shoot him through it would have considerable difficulty in hitting him. "Yes?"

Mumble, mumble, mumble.

McBride reached up and pushed the lever operating the slatted air-conditioner vent which took the place of a transom. "What did you say?"

"Do you want me to shout?" Delilah Chandler's voice demanded angrily.

McBride let her in. She was in the kind of negligee you always see film stars shrug into on rising from bed to let the

gas man in. She was just as good-looking as he had remembered her, maybe even a little more so with the negligee,
which was white satin. Her very dark hair was piled high
on her head and her gray-green eyes were as beautiful as a
cat's. The eyes widened a trifle at sight of McBride's gun.
"Do you always welcome visitors that way?"

"Always," McBride said. He leered at her. "That's the
way I keep my virtue." He replaced the safety chain in its
slot, explaining that this would make it harder to run out
on him. "I've just been sitting here wishing for someone
like you."

Delilah's fine patrician mouth expressed displeasure.
"Indeed?"

"Oh, come now," McBride said genially, "don't tell me
this is a business call." His eyes admired her. "Because if it
is, you're hardly dressed for it. Unless," he added somewhat
enigmatically, "you're in the business."

She began to breathe a trifle raggedly, and for just a
moment her eyes hated him. "I didn't come down here
to—"

"Be insulted?"

"No."

"All right, then," McBride said, "I won't insult you." He
dropped the gun in the side pocket of his robe. "What did
you come down here for?"

"I—don't know." And then, quite suddenly, she turned
her back on him and moved with her fine, long-legged
stride over to the fog-shrouded windows. "Yes, I do, too.
I want you to forget some of the things I told you yesterday." She made an impatient gesture. "No, not yesterday.
Night before last."

McBride's laugh was politely skeptical. "Conscience?"

She wouldn't look at him. "Yes."

"Speak no evil of the dead—that sort of thing?"

"Yes."

He crossed the room in three strides and caught her roughly by the shoulders and swung her around. "It wouldn't be because you're all out of alibis for nine o'clock last night, would it?" And as she would have struggled free he held her still more tightly. "If it comes to a choice of my neck or yours, you know whose it's going to be, don't you?"

Presently the stubbornness went out of her body and she lay quiescent against him. "What kind of man are you, anyway?"

"My own," McBride said angrily.

After a while she said, very low, "I have an alibi, but it would be—well, rather embarrassing to have to use it." She lifted her gray-green eyes and let him look at them. "You wouldn't want me to be embarrassed, would you?"

"The hell with that," McBride said. Her eyes bothered him, and the perfume of her hair was like incense in the Temple of Eros. He fought the compelling urge to crush his mouth against hers. "You don't want me to tell the cops that you were jealous as the fiends of hell. You're afraid that with that as a motive, and no alibi to speak of, they might get the idea her broken fingers were a red herring, is that it?" He laughed shortly. "Well, I sort of had the same idea myself."

"I was afraid you would have."

"So you came down here all prettied up to give me the old glamour treatment, eh?" He pushed her from him. "Well, where were you?"

"With Sebastian," she said calmly. "In his apartment." She moved past him and without hurry to the console and poured herself a stiffish drink. "Cyrus is upset enough already. I'm afraid he'd be pretty difficult."

"I can imagine," McBride said. He sat on the arm of a chair, watching her. "Don't you think it's a little foolish to be running around the halls like that? Cyrus might even become difficult about me."

"Cyrus is over in Oakland. Some trouble in one of the shipyards."

McBride licked his lips. "And here we are, just you and I. Cozy, isn't it?" He stood up suddenly, his eyes dark and humid. "What do you know about Sean O'Hara?"

For just a moment she was confused. "Why—why, nothing!"

He waggled an admonishing finger. "Don't lie to me, beautiful. I was watching you the other night when he came into the Stardust Room. You know him, all right."

"Certainly I know him," she said with a trace of her old arrogance. "There's nobody of consequence in California who hasn't gambled across his tables at one time or another."

McBride appeared to accept that at its face value. "That reminds me, how are you and Cyrus fixed for funds lately?"

Her eyes studied him curiously. "So we're back to that again. You never give up, do you?"

"I want the necklace," he said stubbornly. "Besides a couple of other things, it means a fee of ten thousand dollars to me. I'm going to get it."

She shook her head. "Not from me, you're not."

"From somebody," he insisted.

She poured another drink and drank it quickly, as some habitual drunkards do who need the effect but can't stand the taste. "The police have already been through Celeste's rooms, but they may have missed something. I could let you in if you cared to look."

He smiled at her. "That's the second time, baby. You'd like me to think she took it, wouldn't you?"

"Not particularly. It might help to clear up a few things, that's all."

"All right," he said, "I'll be up after a while." He went to the door with her. And then, casually, as he unhooked the chain: "Is that what you wanted the pass-key for, hon?"

Her half smile became fixed and was not a smile at all, but something pretty ugly. "Did I want a pass-key?"

McBride shrugged. "People tell me things, beautiful. All kinds of people—all kinds of things. I never did know why." He opened the door.

Arthur McGillicuddy stood there looking at them with his mouth open. His right hand, poised as though to knock, fell a little foolishly to his side, and behind thick lenses his pale blue eyes were shocked. "Why—uh—"

"Good morning, Arthur," McBride said genially. His manner denied that there was anything unusual about being visited in his rooms by ladies dressed as informally as Delilah. "Mrs. Chandler, this is Mr. McGillicuddy." He took Delilah's arm with a clubby smile. "Mr. McGillicuddy manages the Hotel Trojan. He welcomed me to San Francisco with a dead body in my room."

Delilah disengaged her arm. "I wish," she said coldly, "that it had been two dead bodies, and that one of them was yours." She swished her satin negligee past Mr. McGillicuddy's nose and strode down the hall. Only McBride knew that the stiffness of her back indicated the proverbial wrath of a woman scorned. As far as Arthur McGillicuddy knew, she had not been.

"Come in, Arthur," McBride invited. "Come right in." He watched a slow flush creep up around young Mr. McGillicuddy's ears. "You don't mind my calling you Arthur, do you?"

"I don't mind what you call me," McGillicuddy said. There was just the suggestion of a tremor in his voice, but he was not afraid. He was just keyed up to something that seemed terrifically important to him. He came into the room with an assurance that was a bit startling in one whom McBride had considered a panty-waist. His blue eyes were slightly magnified and very direct. "I don't care what you do or what becomes of you—just so you stay away from Susan Lee."

McBride drew a deep breath. "Well!" He closed the door carefully.

"If I needed any further proof that you are not a fit person for her to associate with," Mr. McGillicuddy continued, eyeing the door significantly, "I just had it."

"Arthur," McBride said gently, "you've got an evil mind." He went over and poured himself a drink with fingers that shook a little. "I'm not defending my morals, you understand, but really—this time—the lady was above reproach. So was I," he added as an afterthought. "I exercised magnificent restraint." He drank the rye neat and in much the same fashion as Delilah. He felt that he was still exercising magnificent restraint. He fixed McGillicuddy with what he hoped was a hypnotic gaze. "Little man," he said, being very careful to enunciate distinctly, "I do not want your

Susan. I myself made it clear to her that I was something of a heel. I even discussed ethics with her, ethics in which you played one of the leading roles." Righteous indignation overcame him, or maybe it was the rye on an empty stomach. "Beyond that I can not—I will not—go."

"I think you will," McGillicuddy said calmly. He had taken off his hat in deference to Delilah—even though he suspected the worst—and his pale blond hair clung damply, youthfully to his well-shaped skull. He sat on the extreme edge of a chair and placed his hat on his knees and regarded McBride seriously, like an adolescent given the gavel for the day at a Rotary Club meeting. "I think perhaps it might be wise for you to leave San Francisco entirely, Mr. McBride."

A little shock ran up and down McBride's frame. Probably a wolf would have been just as astonished if kicked in the teeth by a rabbit. He recalled Frank Morgan's line: "Are you serious?" but somehow it seemed inadequate. There was no doubt that Arthur McGillicuddy was serious. He made a great effort to breathe only through his nose, one-two-three-four, one-two-three-four. Presently he found that he could speak without shouting. "You seem to have something on your mind, Arthur. What is it?"

"Susan," McGillicuddy said promptly.

McBride nodded. "And what else?"

"Your alibi for nine to ten last night. It's no good," McGillicuddy said. For the first time a trace of nervousness showed in his manner, but he was going through with it. "Call me a snoop, a spy, a jealous moonstruck fool or what you will. I was in the hall outside Susan's apartment when you left. I was still there when you came back."

"I see," McBride said. Now that he knew the worst; knew exactly what he had to cope with, he found that he could view Mr. McGillicuddy in the proper perspective. "If I don't leave town you'll tell the police what you know?"

"Yes." The younger, slighter man spread his hands in a rather pathetic gesture. "I can't compete with a man like you, McBride. The only thing I can do is eliminate you."

Feeling something more of a heel than usual, McBride offered a bribe. "I've still got some business to take care of up here, Arthur. Would a—say a thousand dollars affect your memory?"

"No."

"Two thousand?"

"Nor ten," McGillicuddy said stoutly.

McBride was surprised. He said so out loud. "I'm surprised at you, Arthur, I really am. Ten grand would go a long way with a girl like Susan." Not that he had had any intention of giving McGillicuddy the ten grand. One maybe, but not ten. He resorted to the velvet-coated bludgeon. "Have you thought what it would mean to Susan if you exposed me? They can hand you quite a rap for perjury."

"I'll take care of Susan, thank you."

McBride's teeth shone briefly in a smile that was a little strained at the corners. "I'm sure you will, Arthur." He crossed to the hall door and opened it. "Good-by now."

"Then you won't go?"

"I'll think it over," McBride promised. The smile was still on his lips when he closed the door and leaned his back against it. Presently he discovered that he was panting as though he had just run a hard mile with leg-irons on.

14

SHAVED, BATHED AND looking rather well in a suit of blue-gray Harris tweeds, McBride was breakfasting in the coffee shop off the main lobby and regretting the war's effect on waitresses—they all seemed to be middle-aged, frumpy and bow-legged lately—when he became aware of the brownish gentleman he had met in the Federal Building, Mr. W. Patrick. Without a preliminary word of any kind W. Patrick pulled out the chair opposite McBride and sat down. From a hovering waitress he ordered tomato juice and tabasco. He then lit a cigarette, a brown one to match the rest of him, and blew a perfect smoke ring at one of the lighted chandeliers dependent from the slightly rococo ceiling. "Nothing particular you want to tell me, I suppose?"

McBride glared at him. "I thought you guys were working on that shipyard fire over in Oakland."

"We are," W. Patrick said.

McBride sighed. "All right, I did it." He lifted a hand as the waitress came back with the brown man's tomato juice. "No, don't bother to call out the National Guard. I'll go quietly."

W. Patrick smiled paternally on the slightly goggle-eyed waitress. "My young friend is feeling a trifle ebullient this morning."

Her mind focused on the second syllable of what was—to her—an extremely suggestive word. "I could tell," she said darkly. "I could tell by the way he looked at me." She shivered, rustling her heavily starched uniform. "It fairly made my skin crawl, it did." Fascinated by McBride's alleged effect on her she retreated to the security of a table where practically a whole ship's complement of officers were noisily breaking their fast.

McBride gave her a particularly lecherous leer. It faded when he turned his attention to his uninvited guest. "Listen," he said angrily, "I've got enough troubles with having you guys in my hair."

Patrick nodded. "So I hear."

McBride banged his coffee cup down. "Then what the hell do you want this time?"

The brown man appeared to consider that rather carefully. "Funny thing," he said presently, "practically all of this latest series of accidents in our war plants have occurred since you've been following the Chandlers." He shook a little more tabasco into his tomato juice. "Do you wonder that we're interested in you?"

McBride's mouth drooped. "What the hell am I supposed to have done—gotten Chandler drunk and pumped him dry of state secrets?" He shook his head. "Sorry, chum; Cyrus and I haven't been quite that friendly. Fact is, he tried to kill me last night—I won't tell you why, but it wasn't over war contracts."

"This adopted daughter of his," Patrick said casually. "She may have had access to vital information. What was your opinion of her?"

"I can't tell you without being obscene," McBride said.

So garnishing his opinion with obscenity he offered as his belief the thought that Celeste would have sold anything, including her virtue, for any reasonable sum. "The trouble with that theory is that if she'd had any information she'd have sold it. She wouldn't have had to be tortured. Matter of fact, and presuming that you haven't just been reading spy stories, Celeste would have been quite an asset to a sabotage ring. They'd hardly have killed her, would they?"

W. Patrick agreed somberly that it didn't seem likely. He helped himself to a piece of McBride's toast and nibbled it. "I've been letting you go along, hoping that in pursuit of one thing you might turn up something else." He sighed. "In a way, you too, were an asset. You had a reason for being, whereas my own men were slightly handicapped. We couldn't watch the Chandler menage too closely without tipping off our interest." He finished his tomato juice and made a wry face. "A ticklish business, keeping an eye on our own officials. They get insulted."

McBride thought of something. "I didn't tell you this before because it didn't seem pertinent, but the guy that first tipped me to your college boys was the consul, or an attache to the consulate, of Para. He thought they were my assistants."

"Sebastian?" Patrick shook his head. "We've checked on him, just the same as we checked on you. More quietly, of course, because it was you who forced the issue in your case." He found another of his brownpaper cigarettes and lit it. "Sebastian—even if we had found a connection, which we haven't—has not been out of San Francisco during the whole period. These—ummm—accidents have occurred all the way from Los Angeles to Seattle and back again. Usually *after* Chandler had left."

"Then really you haven't got a thing on them?"

"Not a thing," the brown man admitted. "No more than we have on the thousand and one other possibilities." His firm lips contrived a bleak, sort of frustrated smile. "We just try to plug the loopholes one at a time."

McBride, remembering his own notable unsuccess with Washington, was unsympathetic. "That's what you get for relying on higher education. What you need is some guys with fists and no ethics." He waved for the waitress but she refused to come any nearer.

W. Patrick said, "That reminds me, how are your own efforts coming along?"

"Fine," McBride said. He was moved to a vast pity for himself. "My suspects are dying like flies all around me." With a magnificent prodigality he laid a five-dollar bill on top of the marmalade, pressing it down only slightly, so the waitress wouldn't get her fingers too awfully messy. "Like flies." He stood up. "Well, it was sweet of you to look in on me like this." He went out to the main lobby and caught an express elevator to the fourteenth floor.

In the corridors a few guests were in evidence, not many. The smell of warm food and excellent coffee still lingered in the air, apparently from the recent passing of some waiter trundling his cart to breakfasters-in-bed. The hall lights were all on, for this fog was a persistent one, and the windows were no more good than sheets of butcher's paper. Before 1440-A McBride paused and examined the corridor on either side of him with the caution born of suspicion. Though there was no reason to suppose that this meeting with Delilah was going to be more momentous than the others, it was getting so that he was suspicious of his own shadow, and this worried him a little, for nerves and precise coordination do not usually go hand in hand. Beneath his vest the smaller of his guns lay comforting against the flat hardness of his belly. He knocked.

Delilah let him in almost at once. She had changed to a tailored frock of some light-green material and her feet were slender and patrician in green suede sling pumps with polished wood heels. The ensemble made her fine eyes more green than gray. "I'd about given you up," she said.

McBride looked at her. "Still sore at me?"

"Why should I be?"

The faultless tailoring of the Harris tweeds made his shrug almost as good as one of Rodriguez Sebastian's. He noted the effect in the rose mirror over the fireplace. He was slightly indignant because twenty dollars a day hadn't gotten him a fireplace too. And then, laughing suddenly, he caught her in his arms and kissed her warmly on the mouth. "Now are you satisfied?"

With perfect composure she freed herself. "In a way." Her green eyes were cool and without any suggestion of the fires he felt lay somewhere behind them. "Who was the rabbit you introduced me to?"

"I told you," McBride said. He thought of his own comparison of Arthur McGillicuddy with the Easter bunny. "God save us from guys in love." He was impelled to deliver a short dissertation on love. "It makes mountains out of molehills and tigers out of mice."

Delilah's laugh was tinkling ice in a glass. "But it never affects you, does it?"

"Oh, I don't know," McBride said. He regarded her intently. "You could affect me like anything." He wondered what she was going to do about her husband and Sebastian, now that Celeste was no longer any competition. It occurred to him that her alibi for last night offered one equally for Rodriguez; it also occurred to him that maybe that was the general idea behind this whole set-up. Suppose that one or the other—or both—had killed Celeste, an alibi would be the first thing they'd think of. Inevitably that train of thought carried McBride back to his recent conversation with Mr. W. Patrick of the FBI. Suppose it were Delilah, not Celeste, who had been passing information along to the South American-where did that leave you? It left you no place, that's where. On account of then there would have been no reason for them to kill Celeste. Delilah wouldn't even have been really jealous, for she would have been on the inside track with the Sheik of Para. McBride tossed the whole business in the discard, because none of it seemed to have the slightest bearing on the Adelphi necklace.

Delilah said caustically, "I do hope I'm not boring you." She went into one of the bedrooms, reappearing presently with a green suede purse from which she extracted a key. The key had no tag, no identifying mark of any kind. She held it out. "I was assured that this would open anything in the St. Mark except the safe."

McBride looked at it but did not touch it. "Mind telling me what you wanted it for?"

"Not a bit." Her eyes were clear and direct and suddenly as hard as green ice. "I wanted an uninterrupted look at Celeste's things. I told you how I felt about her. It would

have given me infinite pleasure to find you were right about
her and the Adelphi."

"And did you?"

"No."

"But you think I might?" McBride persisted.

Delilah's shrug rippled the shiny green of her gown.
"Suit yourself. You're supposed to be a detective. I'm not. I
was just trying to help you, that's all."

"All right," McBride said. Still he did not take the key.
"Let's you and I have a look together."

"Do you mind going alone?" Delilah seemed impatient rather than nervous. "It's just across the hall, but I'm
expecting a phone call and I should hate to miss it."

"Leave your door open."

She was frankly laughing at him now. "Still suspicious of
me, darling? Afraid I've baited some kind of a trap for you?"
And when he did not answer she made a half-amused,
half-petulant gesture. "Very well, come on." She opened
the door, glanced up and down the hall, crossed it and
unlocked the opposite door and flung it wide. Over her
shoulder McBride saw a twenty-foot living-room very
similar to his own. It was empty. Three other doors leading
from it were partially open. Delilah's hurried breathing was
the only sound in the stillness. "Satisfied?"

McBride did not know why he shouldn't be, but he was
not. He took the gun out of his waistband. "After you,
baby." He went in rather quickly behind her, holding her
arm with his left hand, pushing her toward the center
of the room. She offered no resistance and presently the
tension went out of him and he released her. Through the
partially open doors he could see an elaborate bathroom,

a dressing-room and a bedroom. Apparently they were untenanted.

Across the hall Delilah's phone began to ring. Her green eyes asked his permission to go answer it. "All right," he said. He followed her to the door and closed it behind her, snapping the night latch. He put the gun in his pocket and began a methodical search of the apartment. He was bending over a fitted dressing-case that had already been rifled at least once when he heard a slight sound behind him. All his teeth were suddenly on edge and his nerve ends jumped, but he did not immediately turn toward the sound. Instead he straightened slowly; in the glass of a framed print over the bed he saw reflected the figure of a man rising from behind the divan in the living-room. The man's right hand was half raised and in it was about the biggest gun McBride had ever seen outside of an armory.

McBride stepped sideways and backward, so that the man was no longer reflected in the glass from the new angle. He took his own gun out and faced the living room door, waiting. From beneath the bed something which he later identified as a pair of hands came out and clutched his ankles, and jerked and flung him headlong into the path of the oncoming man from the living room. He knew that he fired once; then someone stepped on his gun wrist and someone else fell on top of him. A furious but brief and almost silent struggle ensued; a struggle which could have but one ending. When McBride himself realized this he became a possum and relaxed. Through a slitted eyelid he saw two pairs of feet and legs and there was a guy still on top of him. He saw one of the feet lift and aim a kick at his head, made one last heroic effort to avoid it and was completely unsuccessful. A salvo of sixteen-inch guns exploded inside his skull and shocked him into insensibility.

15

THE GRANITE CLIFF that was Sean O'Hara sat blank-faced and unbending beyond the expanse of polished brown beach that was the top of his enormous walnut desk. McBride, whose head felt as though he had been butting it against an even harder cliff than O'Hara, sagged limp and inert in a deep leather chair opposite, a battered hulk, a prisoner before the bar of what Sean O'Hara considered justice. Two of the men who had escorted McBride out here to El Rancho Verdugo had vanished, dismissed by O'Hara. The two others, including the gorilla Bogey, whose head unfortunately had turned out to be harder than Butch Larsen's cobblestone, would have been happy during the Spanish Inquisition. They had been working on McBride for half an hour now, off and on, and it seemed to him that if they hadn't medical degrees they should have. They knew all about the human anatomy and its vital spots. Resting from their latest efforts they regarded him with a clinical interest.

"You gotta kind of admire him," Bogey said grudgingly, and his helper said, "Yeah, he's tough." Presently he said, "Tough but foolish." He bent down and peered into McBride's eyes. "Look, soldier, why don't you give yourself a break?"

McBride lifted a leaden-weighted arm and attempted

to drive his fist into the man's face. He didn't even come close. The effort made the room go round like a pinwheel.

O'Hara's inflexible voice said, "Give him a drink."

McBride rolled his head in stubborn refusal. A hand seized his hair and held his head against the back of the chair. Somebody else thrust the neck of a bottle between his teeth. Rather than lose the teeth he drank. The liquor ran like liquid fire through his body. He had a fit of coughing.

When that was over and his vision had cleared he saw that O'Hara had lighted a cigar. Sunlight came in through slitted Venetian blinds and touched the big man's head with silver. The morning's fog had vanished this side of San Bruno. O'Hara said in a reasoning tone, as to a child, "You see how important this cab driver is to me, don't you, McBride?"

"No."

"He brought you out here," O'Hara said. "He saw the girl. He helped you take her away." Gray eyes examined the gray ash on the tip of his cigar. "So now she's dead and it's no particular secret that she didn't die of old age. The hacker will wonder about that, don't you think?"

"Unless I tell him not to," McBride said. This was purely wishful thinking. He had not seen Butch Larsen since yesterday and he had no reason to suppose that he would ever see him again. Still, if O'Hara considered Butch so important, McBride, from the opposite end of the telescope, could pretend to consider him important, too. As a matter of fact Butch could be very important indeed, but only so long as O'Hara's gorillas didn't know who he was and where to find him. McBride felt that Butch's anonym-

ity was one of the few things that stood between him,
McBride, and an early grave.

O'Hara said, "You should have taken my offer and gone
to Reno, Rex. We'd have avoided all this." The implica-
tion was that "all this" was hurting him worse than it did
McBride. He laid his cigar carefully in an ash tray and
leaned forward across the desk. "We were interrupted in
our conversation last night." He frowned a little, recalling
the interruption. "What did Celeste Chandler tell you
about me?"

"That she owed you some money."

"Nothing else?"

"No."

O'Hara's chair complained under his great bulk. "You
didn't think it funny that I'd try to collect in that way?"

"Maybe."

O'Hara let that ride for a moment. "Why didn't you tell
the cops about it last night?"

"I didn't have to," McBride said. He found that a little
strength was coming back into his body; not enough to
battle three men and get to the door, but the fact that he
still had recuperative powers was encouraging. "A friend
of mine gave me an alibi."

"Then it wasn't you who killed Celeste?"

"No."

"Who did?"

"You," McBride said.

Bogey hit him across the bridge of the nose with a
short length of garden hose. Everybody took time out till
McBride could see again. "I'm surprised at you, clingin' to

ideas like that," Bogey said. "That's the kind of talk helps fill our cemeteries."

McBride had read an article recently, dealing with the anatomy of torture; not with the purely physical aspects, but with the effect upon the mind. It seemed to him that now he had reached the point attained by the subject under discussion. His body was impervious to pain, his mind freed of the fear of it, and he was able to see things with a clarity of vision that was almost startling.

He said distinctly, "It wasn't Delilah. It wasn't a plant. I thought for a little while that it was, but I was wrong." Physically, he was numb; a body temporarily amputated from the mind. Mentally he was a giant. "You guys weren't a set-up arranged by Delilah to get me. I was just a by-product. You were looking for something else."

"What?" That was O'Hara speaking. He was just a face suspended in mid-air. Bogey and the other man were nothing but shadows on the carpet.

"The Adelphi," McBride said with utter certainty. "Maybe something else too, but I'm sure about the necklace. Celeste took it originally; she gave it to you as a pledge against the money she owed you. Then somebody heisted your joint and got it. You thought it was Celeste-or at least a mob hired by her. Then the original theft was discovered." McBride's laugh was a mirthless cackle in his own ears. "You were in something of a spot, weren't you, Sean? Without the necklace you didn't have anything. With it— if you were caught with it—you were even worse off. You'd be convicted of stealing it." McBride thought this was a hell of a joke.

"So I killed her?" O'Hara said.

"Unh-hunh."

O'Hara shook his great head. "You killed her." He was regretful but firm. "It all adds up, McBride. You copped her off out here; you put the squeeze on her until she confessed; you found out where she had the stuff. Then you killed her."

"And I was looking for this stuff when your boys picked me up?" He discovered with some surprise that he could lift his right arm. He wiped his bruised mouth on the back of a hand. "Why the hell should I be hunting for it if she told me where it was? Why did I have to knock her off?"

"Because," O'Hara said grimly, "the Adelphi wasn't enough for you any more." He thrust his chair violently backward and came to his feet. "God damn it, that's why you didn't spill to the cops about me! You wanted me out where you could put the bite on me for the rest of the stuff."

McBride remembered that Slugs Foley and Marge had also spoken of the necklace as though it were only a part of what they were looking for. He said carefully, "Look, Sean, maybe if we got together on this thing—" He saw that he wasn't getting anywhere along this line and he said, "So help me Christ, Sean, I don't know about anything but the Adelphi."

O'Hara suddenly towered above him. "Don't give me that crap, McBride. You've got the stuff. I want it." He made a fist of his great right hand. "I'll tell you something else I want—I want the name of this lousy hack driver. I'll be God damned if I'm going to take a murder rap.

McBride licked his lips. "Meaning that no matter what happens I'm not going to be around to see it?"

"You brought it on yourself," O'Hara said in a flat hard voice. "I gave you the opportunity to get out from under and you wouldn't take it. You and this hacker aren't going to belch—ever."

McBride braced himself for what he knew was coming. "Then I haven't got anything to lose," he said. "The hell with you." He did not even lift a hand to ward off O'Hara's fist.

16

THERE WAS A terrific roaring in his ears, and a sense of
rushing upward through dark illimitable space; curiously,
there was also a feeling of constriction, the darkness having
substance and weight. When he came fully awake it was
suddenly, like a diver breaking water after being released
at some tremendous, unheard-of depth. He was surprised
to see that the sun was still shining. It came in through a
narrow, cobwebbed window set high up in a concrete wall
and laid a lemon-yellow path across a dusty concrete floor.
On a kitchen chair in the path of sunlight sat the gorilla
Bogey. His face was sullen and heavy and intent, and his
eyes pried at McBride's eyelids like fingers, seeking to open
them and find consciousness in the brain behind them, so
that he could resume his work. There was no impatience
about the man's waiting; he just didn't want time wasted,
that was all.

McBride played a little game with himself, counting the
minutes he could stay awake without Bogey finding it out.
His right hand, close to his side and thus invisible to Bogey,
identified the thing on which he lay as a canvas folding cot.
He made his breathing slow and regular and painful, the
painful part being no difficulty at all, for his body ached as
though the bones themselves had been bruised. He listened
for some evidence of another presence in the room, some

sign that he and Bogey were not alone. He could hear none. In his nostrils was the chalky smell of dust, and the faint, sickly-sour smell of wine which has turned to vinegar. He could visualize drinking some of the spoiled wine, anything to take this accursed dryness from his mouth. His jaws ached with the effort of keeping them closed, of not licking his lips, because that would tip Bogey off that he was conscious. His tongue furtively explored the back of his teeth. He was surprised to find that the teeth were all there.

So close that it seemed to be almost inside the room a man's voice said, "How's he doing?"

Bogey did not remove his eyes from McBride's face. "All right."

"I wish I had a drink."

"So do I," Bogey said. Though McBride could not see it, it was obvious that a door separated the two men. After a while Bogey said, "O'Hara tell you where he was going?"

"No."

"Me neither," Bogey said.

Somewhere in the stillness a rat gnawed on wood.

Lying there, not planning on anything, because there seemed so little use in it, McBride pretended that the rat was his mind. He let it nibble tentatively at the problem of Sean O'Hara rather than at his own. His own problems were apparently all solved very neatly. He had nothing more to worry about.

It was fun, though, to imagine O'Hara looking for Butch Larsen among the hundreds of hackers in the Bay area. Bogey could not even swear to the color of Butch's cab. McBride wondered which of all the people connected with Celeste Chandler now had the Adelphi necklace. Delilah,

perhaps? He liked to think that in spite of the fact that
Delilah had not, after all, lured him into O'Hara's net, she
might nonetheless have lifted the stones. He did not like
Delilah Chandler very well. He wondered if O'Hara had
gone to try a little persuasion on her.

After a while it occurred to him that maybe O'Hara was
on the level. Maybe he had not been the one who killed
Celeste. It seemed reasonable that the gambler would have
made sure she wasn't lying before taking any action so
definite as death. Same like he was doing with McBride.
Or maybe he had made a mistake with Celeste and was
nurturing McBride more carefully.

Still, there was the man called the Deacon to consider.
And Marge, bereaved by the sudden passing of Slugs Foley.
Either or both could have finally come into their own—or
what they conceived to be their own. They'd had the stuff
once; at least their associate, Seversky, had had it. Witness
Mr. Sigmund Loeb's testimony that the Adelphi had been
offered him by Seversky. That they had lost it—that Slugs
Foley and Marge had lost it—was attested by their quest
of McBride, whom they thought had taken it from Severn.
But Marge might have recovered it by way of Celeste. So,
too, might the Deacon. It was possible that, as O'Hara
had said, Celeste had employed the quartette—Seversky,
Foley, Marge and the Deacon—to stage the raid on O'Hara's Los Angeles headquarters. If that were true, Celeste
could somehow have managed to cross them up afterward.
Her death could have been a matter of reprisal as well as
recovery of the loot.

On the whole, though, McBride liked to think that there
was still an unknown element somewhere. The pattern was

like that of a crap game in which you said, "If I make this pass I'll let it ride," and you did make the pass, and maybe another, and then suddenly up jumped the devil and your whole system was busted higher than a kite. He wondered if the man who had so persistently interested himself in Celeste, Mr. Rodriguez Franz Sebastian, might not be the South American in the woodpile; the devil who so inconveniently jumped up and disarranged the whole pattern. Had Celeste really been as afraid of him as she pretended? Why? Was his interest something more than that of a rather personable suitor?

And then, quite suddenly, McBride saw Mr. Sigmund Loeb as a prospect. The diamond merchant was certainly aware of the Adelphi. He had admitted one rendezvous with Seversky, alias Severn. He had admitted knowing the Deacon. Was it unlikely that he had also known Celeste? If in no other way, he could have found out about her through Seversky, before knifing that gentleman in the back. Against this you had the undeniable fact that Loeb had thought McBride possessed the necklace. Well, what the hell? Slugs Foley had thought so too—and the police and O'Hara. The only people so far not suspected by one or the other faction were the police. McBride wondered idly if maybe he hadn't been giving Lieutenant Orsatti too much credit as a misguided but honest cop. Maybe Orsatti had the stuff.

Almost unconsciously the fingers of his right hand had been brushing the accumulation of dust on the canvas cot along his thigh until he had quite a little pile of it. Becoming aware of this as a somewhat nebulous but not impossible weapon, he tried to add to his store from the encrusted wall at his side. From behind slitted eyelids he watched the man Bogey. Bogey was becoming a little restless now. Outside, beyond the door, the other man's feet crunched on loose gravel. The gnawing rat paused to listen.

McBride let every ounce of tension go out of his muscles; only his mind was coiled, tight as a wound spring, and fixed on the bulge behind the breast pocket of Bogey's unbuttoned coat. He allowed himself a long, fluttering sigh, opened his eyes, shuddered realistically, closed them again. Bogey was on his feet instantly and in the space of two short breaths was bending over the cot. "Well, pally, it's about time."

McBride mumbled incoherencies.

Bogey bent closer and put both hands on McBride's shoulders. "Here we go again, baby. Snap out of it."

McBride flung the handful of powder-fine dust smack into the guy's eyes. From the effect it could just as well have been pepper. A yell of pure agony escaped Bogey's lips and the clutching hands on McBride's shoulders left them and went to outraged eyes. Somewhere beyond McBride's range of vision the door banged inward and a voice wanted to know what went on. Bogey plunged downward across McBride's body, pinning him to the cot, but he was still blinded. McBride's groping fingers finally got the gun at the same instant Bogey's big hands fastened on McBride's throat. McBride brought the gun out and around over Bogey's arm and struck him again and again in the face.

When he felt the pressure on his throat lessen ever so slightly he gave Bogey a knee in the groin and stood up, clutching the big man to him and using him as a shield against the man in the doorway. This guy had a gun and was dying to use it, but when he finally did it turned out that he was not so good a shot as he thought he was. His first slug passed under McBride's arm and lost itself somewhere in the heaving hulk that was Bogey. McBride's remnant of strength was ebbing fast and he knew he couldn't go on indefinitely holding up a second body between his own and the sniper in the door. He attempted to use the gun in his left hand. He got off one wild shot which did nothing but precipitate a whole volley of shots from the other guy. Bogey suddenly sagged against him, dead weight, and bore him to the floor. It seemed to him that echoing the sound of his fall there was another sound, a sort of cross between a groan and a gusty sigh.

He crawled out from under Bogey and saw Butch Larsen standing there in the doorway where so recently had stood a man with a gun. The man with the gun was now flat on his face on the floor. In Butch's right hand was something that looked like the grand-daddy of all monkey wrenches. On his face was the ferocious triumph of his Viking ancestors. "I guess that'll teach him a lesson," he remarked smugly.

McBride discovered that he was giggling like an idiot. He seemed to have no control over it, nor of the trembling in his arms and legs, and presently he went rubbery all over and sagged heavily to the floor. He was not unconscious. He was perfectly aware of Butch approaching, and of Butch's strong hands on him, but for a little while he was utterly incapable of anything approximating coordination. He was a dish of Jello in the hands of a nervous waitress.

Butch said worriedly, "Look, chum, them other guys

ain't gonna like us a little bit for this. We better scram outa here."

"In a minute," McBride said. Through clenched teeth he dragged air deep into his lungs, methodically, like they tell you to do to overcome nausea. After a time the cramp went out of his jaws and he was better. He found that he could even pull himself erect by using Butch's frame like a ladder and going up hand over hand. It was only after he was actually on his feet that Butch lent him an arm and guided him wobbling towards the door. "You see how it is, pally," Butch said. "I gotta see how far you're gone, on account of if it's too far I'm gonna have a body to explain."

"Sure," McBride said. He kept on putting one foot before the other, carefully, as though he were walking a fence. As they came opposite the second guard he saw that the man was stirring a little. Butch's wrench had not finished him. He steadied himself on Butch's arm, lifted his right foot, aimed it like a man sighting a catapult and kicked the guy in the teeth. "To remember me by," he said thickly. They went out into bright afternoon sunshine and across the graveled yard and through a whispering eucalyptus grove to a dirt road where Butch's car was parked.

The car was a Mercury sedan, not a public hack. Helping McBride in, Butch explained that it was his day off. "I'm hearing this dame we snared outa here yesterday has got herself knocked off permanent, so I think I'd better drop around and see you about it." He started the car. "That's how come I happen to see these four lugs haul you outa the St. Mark freight elevator."

The sunlight hurt McBride's eyes. He squinted them against it. "So you tagged along."

"Well, Jesus," Butch said, "what would you want me to do—call copper?" He was indignant. "Or maybe I should've taken the four guys with my fists!"

"You did fine," McBride said.

Butch shot him a sidelong glance. "They must've worked you over pretty bad, hunh?"

"Bad enough," McBride agreed.

"We'll get you a sawbones."

"No," McBride said. After a while he said, "A Turkish bath, maybe, but no doctor."

"I know the very place," Butch said. He swung the car into a cross artery that presently brought them down to the Bay Shore road. The rush of wind from the open window stung a little color into McBride's face. He opened his mouth wide and let the cold sharpness of it flow into his lungs. Butch said, "The fog helped cover me till we was almost out to Burlingame and by that time, o' course, I knew where we was headed." He took both hands off the wheel and used them in a wide gesture. "But what could I do? I still couldn't call copper, could I? I didn't know what gave. I still don't." He shook his head sadly. "All I'm sure of is that O'Hara has got you, somehow, connected with snatchin' the dame outa his cellar. For all I know, he'll wise to me next."

"You did fine," McBride said again.

Angry color dyed the hacker's neck. "So you don't want to talk!"

McBride looked at him. "At least half of what I took was for just that, friend. I didn't want to talk—about you."

"Well, Christ—"

"Not that that makes us even," McBride said. "I'll make it up to you."

"Forget it."

They began to buck Sunday afternoon traffic and it was four o'clock when they went down marble steps to the Turkish baths that Butch knew about on O'Farrell Street.

At six o'clock McBride came up the same steps, alone, smelling slightly of rubbing oil and liniment but feeling pretty good and looking, except for a certain puffiness about the mouth and eyes, almost normal. The attendants had even managed to rejuvenate his clothes.

In a bar on California Street he had a couple of drinks and read the headlines in the early editions of the Monday morning papers. There was nothing new on the death of Celeste Chandler. McBride was surprised. It seemed to him that he had been away for a long time, at least a couple of weeks. The inquest on Seversky was still set for tomorrow. Slugs Foley wasn't even mentioned. Paying off for his drinks McBride asked the bartender what was new on the radio.

The guy was an oldster with very white hair and puckery skin that looked as though it had stood a lot of weathering. He made an inelegant sound with his mouth. "We just lost a battle in the Solomons." He looked at McBride with angry blue eyes as though McBride were responsible. "The same one they told us we won yesterday."

McBride said, "Well, maybe we'll win it again tomorrow," and went out and began climbing the hill towards the St. Mark. The street lights were on now, and some of the display windows and signs. Out over the bay the night was clear of fog, and glittering diamond necklaces that were the endlessly flowing headlights of cars marked the two bridges. The air was sharp and clean and cold. McBride decided that he had better look in at his rooms, if for nothing more than a topcoat.

At the desk he inquired for phone calls. There had been one from Susan, two from Los Angeles. He was to call a Mr. Erin Rourke and a Miss Kay Ford. The assistant manager who had given him first chance at O'Hara's cancelled suite came out of one of the offices behind the counter, apparently in response to a buzz from the clerk. "May I speak to you a moment, Mr. McBride?"

"Unh-hunh."

They went down to the end of the counter. The houseman was embarrassed. "There are some men waiting in your rooms. I couldn't very well—uh—stop them."

McBride stood perfectly still for a moment. "Cops?"

"Yes."

"They happen to say what they wanted?"

"No." The manager shrugged. "They won't like it if they know that I told you, but after the—the little affair of last night, the St. Mark feels that it owes you something."

"That's all right," McBride said. "I won't tell them." Turning away he said, "Thanks" rather absently and crossed to the elevators and rode up to his floor. Approaching the door he was careful to jingle his room-key, and he was even whistling a little when he unlocked the door. He was properly surprised to see Lieutenant Orsatti sitting on the living-room divan. "Well!"

With his rump on one chair and his feet on another Orsatti's partner looked at McBride as though he too, were surprised. "Hi!" On the floor beside his dangling right hand was McBride's bottle of rye. There was less than two fingers left in the bottom of it. "I hope you don't mind me whiling away the time with a little refreshment?"

"Not at all," McBride said. He came in and closed the door and took off his hat. "It's getting so I feel lonesome without you guys dropping in on me every once in a while." He looked at Orsatti. "What is it this time?"

Orsatti yawned, a difficult feat with a toothpick in your mouth. His jet eyes were still red-rimmed and sleepless and he needed a shave. "The same old sixes and sevens. We thought maybe you might have turned something up."

McBride shook his head. "Not a thing."

Orsatti stretched his short thick legs out in front of him. "Where you been all day?"

"In a Turkish bath over on O'Farrell Street," McBride said. He grinned sheepishly. "I got pretty tight last night."

"Why?"

"Conscience," McBride said.

"You're not kidding anybody on that, either," Orsatti said. He pushed his derby to the back of his head and sat up a little straighter. "You weren't too drunk to know what you were doing?"

"I've never been that drunk," McBride said. His eyes grew bright and watchful. "Come on, Orsatti, let's get this over with. I'm in a hurry."

"All right," Orsatti said. He jerked his round head at his partner. "Show him what we found, Al." He himself did not get up. All he did was take his gun out and hold it in his lap.

Al rose to his feet, looking at McBride from beneath pouchy lids. "In case you've forgotten, it's in the bathroom." He pointed. "After you, chum." He and McBride went through the open bedroom door and into the bathroom. Al looked interestedly at the flush tank behind the toilet. "This is kind of like a Easter hunt, ain't it? Open it up, pal. Take the lid off and see do you find the same things we did."

McBride said, "You son of a bitch."

Al was hurt. "Who, me?"

"If there's anything there, you guys put it there." McBride swiveled as though to go back into the living room. "Orsatti is sore because I hit him, but by God he isn't going to get away with this!"

Al put a beefy red hand in the middle of McBride's chest. "You didn't hit me, chum, and I saw it, too." He pushed, not hard, against McBride's body. "Open her up, chum."

"No."

"All right, then, I'll do it for you," Al said. He moved McBride in ahead of him and lifted the heavy porcelain lid and laid it across the lavatory bowl. He appeared entranced with something at the bottom of the tank beneath the water, but not too preoccupied to lose sight of McBride. "Pretty, aren't they?"

McBride was oppressed with the sudden fear that whatever was down there might just happen to be the Adelphi necklace. He looked. A thousand scintillating pinpoints of light winked back at him, magnified by the water itself. There were diamonds there all right, a cupped handful of rings and trinkets, and one bracelet that looked as though it might bring five or six thousand dollars, but there was no Adelphi. He breathed a sigh of relief. "Well, Al, it looks like you boys have made a find, but it hasn't anything to do with me."

Orsatti appeared silently in the bathroom door. "Then they aren't yours?"

"No."

"That's what we thought," Orsatti said. He nodded at his partner. "All right, Al, fish 'em out and we'll take Mr. McBride for a little walk."

"Now listen," McBride said angrily, "if you think I'm going down to the Hall without a warrant you're crazy!"

Orsatti's eyes were suddenly evil and sadistic. "We've already got a warrant, pal, but this time we've got a better place than the Hall to talk to you in." Fat lips rolled the toothpick to the opposite corner of his mouth. "More private. We can talk for a long time without being interrupted." He laughed his husky whisky laugh. "We can practically talk your ears off, McBride."

McBride had already had one working-over today; he knew he could not stand another. "All right," he said tiredly, "I can't argue with a gun." His shoulders drooped. He waited till Al had flushed the toilet and plunged both arms down into the tank. Then, hip shoving the heavy porcelain lid off the lavatory, pulling Orsatti's eyes and gun down with it, he pivoted and hit Orsatti with everything he had, right on the button. The squat man bounced against the door jamb and caromed into the arms of Al, whom the crash had warned, but not quite soon enough. Orsatti's dead weight flung Al back onto the toilet seat and he was still sitting there embracing his sodden partner when McBride scooped up Orsatti's gun and ran out.

At the desk downstairs he said, "I'll take my envelope from the safe, please." And when he had signed for and gotten it: "I might not be back for a day or two." He went out quietly and without hurry, as though completely unaware that a girl in the telephone exchange was shrieking, "Stop him? Stop whom?"

17

SUSAN LET HIM in with the air of a distrait mother whose sudden relief from worry takes the form of a vast disapproval. "Where have you been all day?"

McBride hung his head and scuffed the carpet with an embarrassed toe. "Just playing, moms."

Susan regarded his face intently. "You've been fighting."

"Well, a little," he confessed.

"Who with?"

"Some other guys," he said a trifle vaguely. He laughed suddenly and caught her to him and planted a rousing kiss on her lips. "Gee, moms, you kiss wonderful."

"You do pretty well, yourself," Susan said. She pushed him away. "You smell of liniment."

McBride pretended surprise. "Is that what it is? Me and the other guys thought it was vermouth. We drank it."

"You're a fool," Susan said severely.

"Well, honest, moms, it didn't have no label on it and we thought—" He saw that she had been genuinely worried and he said, "All right, O'Hara and some of his hoods had ideas about me. They've still got them." Almost absently he added, "That isn't the only reason I can't stay here, though." He told her about Orsatti and the planted diamonds. "They'll have a general alarm out for me pretty soon now. This is one of the first places they'll look."

Susan's eyes searched his face. "Who did it? Who could have put those things there, I mean?"

McBride shrugged. "Your guess is as good as mine, pet." On the fingers of his left hand he began ticking off just a few of the possibilities. "Orsatti himself, Delilah Chandler and/or her husband, a guy named Sigmund Loeb, another guy named Rodriguez Franz Sebastian, you—" He ran out of fingers.

Susan wrinkled her nose and considered herself as a suspect. "You're so clever," she sighed. "I suppose I might as well confess."

"Oh, that isn't all," McBride assured her. "There's lots and lots of others. Maybe Sean O'Hara did it, for reasons known only to himself. Maybe it was a party called the Deacon, or a gal named Marge, or even Arthur McGillicuddy." He frowned. "Though I can't see Arthur throwing away eight or ten thousand dollars' worth of stuff just to get me out of circulation." He told her about Arthur's visit and threat. "The guy thinks I'm a bad influence for you."

Susan was startled. "Arthur did that?"

"Arthur," McBride said, "has suddenly become the male of the species—rampant."

Susan's voice took on a slight edge, as though she might be quite furious inside but was doing her best to restrain herself. "I think I'd better have a heart-to-heart talk with Mr. McGillicuddy."

"No," McBride said. He put a hand under her chin and tilted her head back. "According to his lights Arthur is perfectly right. I am a bad influence for you." He smiled into her eyes. "This last business with the cops will make it unnecessary for Arthur to go to them and expose you as a liar. I wouldn't have let him do it anyway, as a matter of fact, but now there won't be any occasion."

Sudden swift tears came into her eyes. "Then this is good-by?"

"For a while, anyway." His mouth became unpleasant. "If for no other reason than the one I told you. Orsatti has really got something this time. He won't let go of it. He'll put a stake-out on this place and on every other place he thinks I might turn up. You'll have to watch your step, hon."

"But you're not really running away?"

"No." He took out a handkerchief and wiped her eyes and then bent and kissed the lids gently. "You're one of the few women I've known who look all right after crying." He found his hat and put it on. "I don't suppose there were any answers to that ad?" And when she shook her head: "Well, it's a little early yet."

She clung to him. "Will you— Suppose he does call, what shall I do? Where can I get in touch with you?"

"I'll let you know," McBride promised. "If the Deacon does call, you're not Marge, you're just speaking for her. Ask him if there's any place you can have Marge meet him." His eyes grew thoughtful. "He probably won't fall for that one, but you can ask him. And if he wants to talk to her, tell him to call back later-say at ten o'clock. I'll ring you before then." Still holding her in the crook of his arm he reached behind him and opened the door. "Take care of yourself, baby."

"All right," she said in a carefully matter-of-fact voice. The door closed.

McBride stood there for a moment, listening to the normal seven-o'clock sounds that apartment house dwellers make. A man and two women got out of the automatic elevator, looked at McBride without curiosity and disappeared around an ell in the corridor. Somewhere outside in the night, not near enough to indicate its approach to the immediate scene, a police siren was faintly reminiscent of the baying of a bloodhound.

McBride turned and descended by way of a service stairs to a paved alley. Oddly enough, the imminent police dragnet gave him a feeling almost of immunity. While dangerous in itself—indeed if all San Francisco cops were like Orsatti, McBride would probably be shot on sight-it would at least serve to pull the teeth of those two utterly dissimilar gentlemen, Arthur McGillicuddy and Sigmund Loeb. The police were no longer in need of such information as these two possessed; McBride was already on the run, which ought to please little Arthur no end. And if it didn't exactly please Mr. Sigmund Loeb, he would see how ineffectual his threat must now be. You can't very well expose a man already exposed—even by planted jewels. McBride wondered if by chance Mr. Loeb had done the planting himself. There was little or no doubt in his mind that the stuff found in the toilet was part of the loot hijacked from Sean O'Hara—probably an infinitesimal part, especially if you considered the Adelphi necklace—and that someone had been willing to sacrifice the part in order to saddle McBride with guilt for the whole.

It was at this point that McBride was struck with a somewhat amusing thought. The police wouldn't be able to identify the stuff they'd found as stolen, because it had never been reported as stolen. As in the case of the Adelphi it had originally been left in pledge with Sean O'Hara.

And O'Hara himself would be the last one to ask assistance of the police in recovering it. O'Hara liked to take care of these things personally—witness his handling of Celeste Chandler, whom he thought had instigated the heist. McBride was almost certain, now, that she had not; his telephone conversation with the deputy warden at San Quentin had helped him in this belief.

He wished O'Hara—along with a dozen or so others—had been just a little more amenable to reason. McBride had a perfectly lovely theory about how the O'Hara heist had been arranged. The trouble was that nobody would give him a chance to expound the theory. They all wanted to beat hell out of him, or kill him, or scare him out of town. More and more he was impressed with the idea that somebody in this case—the somebody who probably now had the Adelphi—didn't know what the hell he was doing. There was evidence of a running around in circles which almost amounted to panic, but even here you couldn't put your finger on any one particular person as the frantic one.

Little McGillicuddy, for instance, had been frantic, or at least upset, at thought of McBride seducing Susan Lee.

Delilah Chandler feared exposure of her jealousy lest it convict her of killing Celeste, though to be quite accurate this was only her stated reason for asking McBride's silence; she could have had another and more obscure one.

Probably Slugs Foley's gal Marge was frantic, and the Deacon, if for no other reason than that a couple of unexpected murders always complicate things.

And though the gambler Sean O'Hara was not the hysterical type, it was conceivable that Celeste's murder

had him worried; if not the murder itself, then the imminent possibility of being convicted for it.

Always, McBride thought, I come back to that—to
the murder of Celeste Chandler. It's the part that doesn't
fit. O'Hara had, or thought he had, a good reason to kill
her. But he could not have killed Seversky, alias Severn,
because he didn't know about Severn; even had Celeste
hired Seversky and Slugs Foley—now unlikely because of
McBride's other theory—O'Hara could not have learned
about them except through her. And when he had first
grabbed her Seversky was already dead and in the morgue!

At the desk in the lobby of the Manx, McBride bought
a handful of nickels, dimes and quarters and entered a
phone booth. His first call was to the Chandler suite at the
St. Mark. Delilah herself answered and unaccountably he
was relieved. He had no particular reason to love Delilah,
though she kissed rather interestingly. "Remember me,
darling?"

Her gasp of surprise seemed genuine. "What happened
to you? Where have you been all day?"

"Just in case you don't know," McBride said, "I've been
having a little seance with some people I ran into in
Celeste's rooms. Some very tough people." His eyes were
malicious. "They'll be around to see you next, baby."

"To see me?" She sounded a little frightened now. "See
here, Mr. McBride, I hope you don't think—I mean to say,
I had nothing to do with whatever happened in Celeste's
rooms after I left you." He could visualize worry clouding
her gray-green eyes. "Absolutely nothing."

"Whether you did or not," he said, "I suggest that you
take steps to protect yourself. Have your husband get some

of the bright boys from the FBI." His mouth drooped. "Get your lover Sebastian to squire you around—if you just have to go out. Me, I don't think you'd better."

There were clicking sounds from the other end. McBride could not tell whether Delilah's teeth were chattering, her knees knocking or it was just trouble on the line. She said, "But—but why should these—these people wish to harm me?"

"They think you may have, among other things, the Adelphi." He laughed a little. "I don't suppose you have, darling?"

"Certainly not!" And then, after the briefest of hesitations: "Whatever gave them that idea?"

"I did," McBride said. He waited for her to speak, but when a full minute elapsed without a sound he said, "If you've got it you'd better turn it over to me and let me handle these babies. They're tough."

Her voice shook. "Who—who are they?"

His eyes narrowed as he debated telling her about O'Hara. He decided against it. "Your guess is as good as mine, beautiful. All I can tell you is that they're pretty hard to convince." And in a flat, deliberately brutal voice he added, "Remember Celeste? Remember her fingers?"

"Oh God, don't!"

He was inexorable. "You see what you're up against, Mrs. Chandler. If you have the stuff, get rid of it. Let me have it and I'll take the heat off you."

"I can't. I haven't got it, I tell you!"

He thought that she was just frightened enough to be telling the truth. "Does that mean that you never had it?"

She caught her breath, "So help me God!"

"I hope He does," McBride said sincerely. He hung up. After a thoughtful interval he lifted the receiver again and with four quarters bought a short and bitter conversation with Erin Rourke in Los Angeles. "What do you want this time?"

Rourke countered with a question of his own. "What the hell's going on up there? I just called the St. Mark again and they tell me there's a general alarm out for you."

"No!"

"Well, is there or isn't there?"

McBride sighed. "So what if there is? It's my neck, not yours."

A new voice interrupted Rourke's flow of profanity. "Hello, Rex." It was Miss Kay Ford being carefully unemotional. "You hadn't intended calling me, had you?"

"Certainly I intended calling you!"

"Oh, I'm so sorry," Miss Ford said. She was not sorry. She knew he was lying just as well as he did. "I thought perhaps you wouldn't, so I just came over and waited with Mr. Rourke."

McBride was furious. "I'll thank you to mind your own goddam business, darling. I'm getting sick and tired of all this espionage. You'd think we were married!"

"God forbid," Miss Ford said piously. And then in direct contradiction: "When may we expect you home?"

"Never!" McBride shouted.

Miss Ford's tone became that of a smugly omniscient parent. "Is she very lovely, Rex?"

In spite of himself he was startled. "Who?"

"This-this bookkeeper. Susan Lee, isn't it?"

"Never heard of her."

Rourke's voice said, "That's a lie! My informant up there told me—you yourself told me—"

"And you told Kay Ford," McBride said. "How too, too thoughtful of you." Rage like a ball of hot mush welled up in his throat. "Remind me to do something nice for you too, you bastard!"

He was on the point of hanging up when Rourke said, "Now wait a minute, Rex. About the party you asked me to look up-this Deacon. His name is Clyde Clement and he used to work for the Hollywood Park Racing Association."

"Thanks for nothing," McBride said bitterly. "A deputy warden up at San Quentin told me that twelve hours ago.

Rourke was surprised. "Well, guess who got him the job with the track."

McBride had already guessed. "Sean O'Hara."

"Well, for Christ's sake!"

"Think nothing of it," McBride said. After a moment he repeated an observation he had made many times before in connection with the vice-president of West Coast Indemnity. "I don't know what the company sees in you."

Rourke choked on a choice morsel of obscenity. "I'm coming up there and handle this thing myself!"

"Fine," McBride said. "That's just ducky. I'll have the cops and Sean O'Hara's mob and a few of the other boys arrange a reception committee for you." He banged the receiver down, banged out of the booth and strode angrily across the lobby. A uniformed cop was leaning on the desk in earnest conversation with the night clerk. "Name of McBride," the cop was saying, "though he probably won't use it."

18

THE HOUSE WAS like so many of those in San Francisco, even as San Francisco in respect to its houses is like Jersey City. McBride felt that a visit of either city to Southern California wouldn't have done it any harm. All the way out Van Ness Avenue he had been calling to Butch Larsen's attention the tight-packed atrocities whose only concession to modernity was a coat of stucco slapped on the front of an otherwise frame structure. They were like very old women temporarily, but obviously, rejuvenated by Charles of the Ritz.

The address listed as that of Sigmund Loeb was a two-story frame wedged in the middle of a row of two-story frames exactly like it, only they had varied the stucco facial with artificial stone. Over a basement garage bulging bay windows looked down on a street full of excellent cars; cars which suggested that the occupants of the houses had plenty of money to live elsewhere, only they didn't know any better. Narrow, iron-railed steps climbed to a narrow stone stoop between the goggling bay windows. There was light behind drawn shades.

McBride made a disparaging gesture. "Look at it!" He and Butch were both slightly drunk as a result of looking for a suitable place to eat dinner. In each of half a dozen recommended spots they had sampled only the liquid aperitifs before deciding to go elsewhere, each drink making it increasingly difficult to decide, until finally they had ended up at Jacopetti's where they each had a turkey leg, a turkey wing and three sandwiches of white meat sliced by a Chinaman who still wore his pigtail.

Butch said argumentatively, "Well, now, I don't see nothing wrong with it." He felt that as a cab driver he must defend the status of his clientele. "Lots of nobs live around here. I bring 'em home alla time."

"Home!" McBride sneered. "You call this home!" He got out of the car with some difficulty, removed Lieutenant Orsatti's gun from his coat pocket and sighted along its barrel at one of Sigmund Loeb's bay windows. "Who does this kike bastard think he is?"

"Now look," Butch protested, "you promised me there wasn't gonna be no shooting!"

"Am I shooting?" McBride demanded. He eyed Butch's overcoat jealously, for the night had grown colder instead of warmer and Orsatti's visit had precluded obtaining one of his own. "You sure you wouldn't like to lend me the benny?"

"No."

"Nor sell it?" McBride persisted.

"No." For perhaps the tenth time since the subject had first been broached Butch explained that it was Sunday, and that short of stealing one there was no way of replacing the garment in question. "And I won't steal a guy's benny," he said righteously. "His watch, yes. Maybe even his teeth." He shook his head. "But not his benny. Why, I remember once—this was in France in '18—some son of a bitch lifted my coat and I like to froze to death till I found it on a corpse."

McBride stared at him suspiciously. "How'd you know it was yours?"

"Because the guy was wearing two of 'em when I shot him," Butch said. He leaned out of the car and attempted to take the gun from McBride's fist. "Better leave that with me, chum. Then I know there won't be any shooting."

McBride eluded him. "I'll trade you."

"For what?"

"For the benny."

Butch shook his head violently. "No!"

"All right, then," McBride said, "the hell with you. I'll shoot who—whom—I please, when I please." He put the gun back in his pocket and appraised the flight of stone steps he was going to have to climb. "And I hope your lousy coat gets moths in it." He went up the steps, leaning heavily on the iron rail, but only stumbling once. He felt that this was commendable. He commended himself and tried to peer through one of the bay windows, but was unsuccessful because of the drawn blinds. He located and rang the doorbell.

After a moment's wait he found himself looking at a Negro maid. She had a flat, triangular yellow face, plucked eyebrows and wavy, not kinky, auburn hair. In spite of the prim black dress, the prim lace bandeau and apron, there was nothing either prim or servile in the way she stood there and stared at him. She had an arrogant assurance that said she knew what went on; that she had admitted other and stranger callers than McBride. He thought that she must have met plenty of Loeb's sub-rosa associates. He got out his card case and gave her one of the cards with nothing on it but his name. "Take that to your boss, Red."

"I dunno can Mistuh Loeb see you right now." She had a soft voice, low and throaty. "If you was to come back in maybe half an hour."

"Give him the card anyway," McBride said. He leaned comfortably on the iron railing and savored the brisk night air. He thought the turkey was gradually absorbing some of the alcohol in his stomach. "I'll wait." He was not affronted when she closed the door without inviting him in. He found that he could look down on the street even from these great heights without dizziness. He felt fine.

It was Sigmund Loeb himself who presently reopened the door. He was effusive. "Well, well, Mr. McBride, this is indeed a pleasure. Come in. Come right in, sir!" He was in a royal purple dressing-robe with a huge embroidered monogram on the breast pocket. His enormous predatory nose quivered, no doubt scenting a profit. His gray-streaked dark hair was sleek and shiny.

McBride allowed himself to be guided across a surprisingly well-furnished hall and into a living-room whose decorators apparently had decided to just ignore the outside of the house. The walls were paneled in bleached mahogany and pine and the few pictures were good. A comfortable fire burned on the hearth. Before it was a low glass-topped table on which was a carved silver tray containing a decanter, a siphon of soda, a bowl of ice cubes and one glass. On the polished surface of the tray were the marks of two glasses. The chair McBride sat in was still warm from the former occupant. He moved the chair a little so that he could command the room's three doors.

Loeb sat and crossed his knees and leaned his head back against the tall back of his chair. His heavy-lidded eyes were bright and shiny and expectant. "Well sir, Mr. McBride, I never thought to see you again and that's a fact."

McBride looked at the door directly behind his host. It seemed to him that it was not closed as tightly as it could have been. "Why?"

Loeb's laugh was as fat and rich and oily as a dollar Havana. "Well, the police, you know. I must say that I underestimated you, Mr. McBride. I did indeed."

The auburn-haired maid came in without knocking and put fresh glasses on the tray. Her knowing eyes considered McBride slyly and she swayed her lean hips a little as she went out. McBride said, "That baby is going to cut your throat one of these days, Siggy. She's got the eye for it."

Loeb's chuckle ran around the corners of the room. "Beulah is too fond of her own, Mr. McBride." He came forward in his chair and poured pale aromatic Scotch into two of the glasses. With heavy silver tongs he put in ice cubes, and tilted the glasses and ran the soda down the inside slopes with loving care. Mr. Loeb was obviously a connoisseur.

McBride said, "Any more anonymous phone calls, Siggy?"

Mr. Loeb appeared to have some difficulty recalling that he had ever mentioned such a thing. "Anonymous phone calls?" He thought some more. "Oh, you mean that little matter we discussed the other day." His gray eyes massaged McBride's face gently. "The Adelphi, eh?"

"As if we weren't both thinking about it," McBride said.

"So you came down here all prettied up to give me
the old glamour treatment, eh?" McBride asked.

Loeb lifted his glass to the light and admired the amber liquid. "Am I to understand that it is now in your possession?"

"Not on me," McBride said. "I can get it."

"And you wish to sell it to me, is that it?"

"Maybe."

Loeb sighed. "Well, to tell you the truth, Mr. McBride, I'm no longer interested. Circumstances have arisen which would make it a bad investment—even if you had it, which I doubt."

"Circumstances such as what?"

"Too many people have been killed in connection with it," Loeb said carefully. "I should not like to have my name added to the list."

McBride's laugh was a sneer. "You weren't afraid of the cops yesterday."

"Nor am I today," Loeb said, adding thoughtfully, "Though people as hot as you are, I do not like them coming here."

McBride watched the door behind Loeb's chair. "You wouldn't have heard from the Deacon, would you?"

"No."

"I just wondered," McBride said. He was practically cold sober now. "The Deacon would know better than anyone else the kind of people you'd be up against. He used to work for them."

"The Deacon," Loeb said, "was in San Quentin at the time of the Chandler robbery."

McBride stood up. "Then he didn't tell you about it?"

Loeb said, too quickly, "About what?" He attempted to cover up with, "I just told you I haven't seen him."

McBride laughed at him. "I know you did, Siggy, old chum. And I almost know for a fact that he came to you because he thought you might have heard from Marge. He thinks maybe Marge has got the stuff. He's wrong."

Loeb's breathing was beginning to show signs of incipient asthma. "How do you know?"

"Because I've got it," McBride said. He modified the lie a trifle. "At least I know where I can lay my hands on it." He pointed a finger at Loeb's magnificent nose. "And if you and he don't want to do business with me I'll go to O'Hara. O'Hara would pay plenty, not only for the stuff, but for the name of the guy who crossed him."

A sweat as unreal as the glycerine they use in the movies broke out on Loeb's forehead. "How did he— Then it is O'Hara!"

McBride nodded. Catching sight of his own face in the mirror over the mantel he reflected that he might have made a very fine actor. "You saw what he did to Celeste's fingers-or did you?" He shuddered realistically. "He's going to feel terrible when he finds out he got the wrong party."

The door behind Loeb's chair came open and the Deacon himself stood there, pushing a gun at McBride's face. He was even taller and thinner and more funereal than McBride remembered him. He said with the gentleness of a solicitous undertaker, "I don't believe he's going to find that out, friend."

The hall door opened and the Negro maid Beulah, also with gun, looked at McBride with the insolence a Central Avenue nigger gives the hapless white who invades his territory. She said nothing. Her triangular sepia face was quite handsome.

McBride said, with a huge disgust for himself as well as the others, "The more you see of this lousy racket the worse it looks to you. It's dog eat dog and don't be too particular about how long the one you eat has been dead." He made a fine gesture of disdain for their guns. "You might as well put the toys away. You know you aren't going to shoot me, and I know it, because if you do you'll never get the stuff."

He blew out his breath. "Try anything else and I'll make you shoot me."

There was a space of perhaps five seconds in which he thought he might have guessed wrong. If they had the stuff they would shoot; they would have everything to gain and nothing to lose, for all they had to worry about was his threatened disclosure to O'Hara.

They did not shoot.

Loeb's laugh ran around the room like mice in the wainscoting. "I admire you, Mr. McBride, I do indeed. You are a man after my own heart." He turned his head a little and looked at the maid. "Run along now, Beulah."

"Better have her leave the gun," McBride said. "I told you how I felt about her. I'd be afraid to go down the front steps with her at my back."

In a face that was suddenly yellow and strained her eyes hated him.

"Beulah," Loeb said gently.

Without a word she tossed the gun in a chair and went out. McBride looked at the Deacon. "Now yours, Clyde." He shrugged. "Guns always make me nervous, and when I'm nervous I can't talk for sour apples."

Sigmund Loeb sat forward in his chair a little and washed his hands with air. "Talk," he said genially. "Now there is something I like. It costs so little, yet sometimes means so much." He quit washing his hands and used one of them in a gesture to the man in the doorway behind him. "Clyde."

The Deacon came into the room and laid his gun carefully beside Beulah's. His emaciated body was racked by a sudden fit of coughing. He turned his back, but not quite soon enough to hide from McBride the flecks of bloody foam on his lips. "Excuse me."

McBride made an effort to say something and was surprised to find that he couldn't. It occurred to him that there must be extenuating circumstances for almost every-thing.

Loeb got up and pushed a third chair towards the fire, facing it. "Sit down, Clyde." And after a time, more happily, "Now we shall have our little talk, eh?"

The Deacon looked at McBride with the eyes of a sick spaniel. "I don't know how much you have guessed, friend."

McBride lifted his glass and drank thirstily. "It goes something like this," he said presently. "You knew some-thing about O'Hara, something that perhaps only a very few people besides himself were supposed to know." He recalled the somewhat mysterious manner in which Sean O'Hara had reached his office in the place out beyond Burlingame without using any of the visible doors. "I think he must be addicted to secret entrances to all his places. I think that by some freak of circumstances Celeste Chan-dler became aware of this, and O'Hara knew it, and it was this that led him to believe she had arranged to have him knocked over."

The Deacon used a fresh handkerchief to muffle another fit of coughing. He neither denied nor affirmed McBride's conclusions.

McBride looked at Loeb's monogrammed purple robe with intense dislike. "Perhaps this was to be the Deacon's last job; perhaps for reasons of his own he felt himself justified in hijacking an old friend. I wouldn't know about that. All I know is that while he was still in San Quentin he mapped out the heist for a guy named Seversky, who then hired Slugs Foley and maybe Marge to help him carry it through. They went south to Los Angeles and probably by way of the secret entrance caught O'Hara with his pants down—alone in his office and with the safe open. They emptied it out and managed to break clean in spite of a little shooting here and there." He began roaming around the room, picking things up, putting them down again. "The Deacon figured he'd be in the clear with O'Hara because there is no better alibi in the world than a state's prison."

Loeb cleared his throat noisily. "You shouldn't have done that, Clyde." His tone was that of a lenient parent admonishing a child for some slight indiscretion. "Crooks should got to stick together."

The Deacon shivered. "Maybe crooks that expect to live," he said in his patient, emotionless voice. He stared at McBride with sick, faintly apologetic eyes. "They turned me loose a little early to save themselves the expense of burying me." In the stillness his labored breathing was quite audible. "I needed a stake, not for myself, but for someone I am—rather fond of."

Loeb became brisk. "Well, what's done is done. Except for Mr. McBride here, and Foley's woman, there's still nobody to tip O'Hara."

"Marge won't do any talking," McBride said. "Not to O'Hara, anyway."

Loeb's heavy-lidded gray eyes opened wide. "Then what are we waiting for? You got the stuff." His smile was a trifle wolfish. "And personally I don't care how you got it. Maybe you knocked off Seversky and Foley, maybe you didn't." He spread his hands. "All we got to do is arrange terms, no?"

"That's right," McBride agreed. His smile was even more wolfish than Loeb's. He looked at the Deacon. "Even you don't know the extent of the haul, do you?"

The thin man moistened his lips with an infinitesimal sip of Scotch. "No. Seversky was already dead when I got to him." He coughed a little. "I didn't know about the Foleys till afterwards."

"You'd better tell me about that," McBride said. "Was it you that slashed my bag?"

"Yes." After a time, speaking very carefully, as though the words were precious the Deacon said, "I'd arranged to meet Seversky at the Trojan as soon as I got out. The IOUs and the cash were the big things, of course, but I thought there might be some valuable stones, too; so if there were any, Seversky was supposed to get in touch with Sig, here."

Loeb chuckled. "The Adelphi was just plain luck." He pointed a finger at McBride. "Yes sir, just plain astounding luck."

"Wasn't it!" McBride said.

The Deacon had recourse to a handkerchief again. McBride looked away. He rather hoped the Deacon would die before it became necessary to turn him up. The thin man lifted haggard eyes to the dancing flames in the fireplace. Whatever he saw in them for himself he said nothing about. "When I got into San Francisco I telephoned Seversky and he told me we'd done better than I expected. I went up. He wasn't in his room. Waiting, I noticed the open window and thought I heard a sound from the fire escape." He paused for breath. "After a while I went down and found him dead."

Loeb appealed to McBride. "A blow, eh?" He winked. "The poor fellow plans the whole thing and then at the last minute he ain't got nothing. Seversky's gone, the stuff is gone, and he don't know you from Adam's off ox. All he's got is the hope that maybe the Foleys have salvaged something, or maybe knocked off Seversky themselves, and that they will come to me." He chuckled delightedly. "So he comes to me, too."

"Yes," McBride said. "I thought he might." He stared down at the Deacon's bowed head. "I don't suppose you saw my ad in tomorrow morning's papers—about Marge needing you?"

"No."

"I was afraid you wouldn't," McBride said sourly. "Nobody ever reads those goddam personals any more." He went over and picked up the two guns in the chair. "We'd better not leave these lying around. Beulah might decide to murder both of you." He put them in his pockets. With the one he already had they made him look rather untidy.

Loeb came to his feet with surprising agility. "See here, sir, what are you up to? How do we know you'll be back?"

"Figure it out for yourself," McBride said. "I need somebody who can handle the stones, and I need somebody to help me put the bite on O'Hara for those IOU's." He smacked his lips. "Plenty of sugar for all of us, Siggy." At the hall door he turned, his eyes measuring Loeb for size. "How's about lending me an overcoat, old pal, old pal?"

19

FROM A PHONE booth in an Italian fruit store in the Five Points district McBride called El Rancho Verdugo. He had some little trouble getting anyone to admit that they even knew Sean O'Hara, let alone acknowledge that the syndicate head was actually on the premises. Finally he said angrily, "All right, be coy and see what it gets you! If I don't hear from O'Hara in five minutes I'm going to break an invariable rule about keeping my mouth shut." He hurled the number of the booth phone into the mouthpiece and banged up the receiver.

Leaving the door open he went out and bought an unripe banana from the Italian proprietor and ate it. He bought and ate a persimmon too, though he was as particular about getting the persimmon ripe as he had been about the firmness of the banana. He had once eaten a green persimmon and recalled that he had been unable to talk distinctly for some little time afterward. He thought he was going to have to do some serious, not to mention fast talking in the next hour or so. He and the Wop discussed Joe Di Maggio, and Joe's family and Mussolini and one thing and another until the phone rang. He went into the booth and closed the door.

O'Hara was still being cagey. "Who is this, please?"

"J. Edgar Hoover!" McBride snarled. "Listen, you Irish

bastard, don't get the idea I love you. I just need you, that's all, and by God I'm going to get you or I'm going to sing pretty for the cops!"

"You couldn't prove a thing."

"The hell I couldn't," McBride said. "I've got a witness that saw Celeste Chandler crawl out of your cellar window. The same witness saw your boys cop me off; in fact it was his monkey wrench that laid your gorilla cold—the one that wasn't already dead, I mean."

O'Hara took his time digesting this information. "Then it wasn't you that shot Bogey?"

"Hell, no; I was just using him for a shield. The other guy had a nervous trigger finger."

"That isn't all he's got," O'Hara said bitterly. His voice became smooth and casual. "Who was the guy with the wrench—that hack driver?"

McBride cursed him. "Listen, I'm not going to have this lug worrying about an ambush for the rest of his life. He won't talk, and I won't—provided we can get together and clean this thing up." He drew a deep breath. "If we can't, there's one hell of a good way for me to get out from under the Chandler kill. I'll toss you to the cops instead."

O'Hara's voice took on an edge. "I'm a bad man to threaten, Rex."

"Bad!" McBride sneered. "Christ, you're not bad. You let a couple of punks walk in on you down South and practically wheel the safe out." Through the glass door of the booth he kept a watchful eye on the front of the store. It was possible that O'Hara had traced the phone number and already had some of his boys on the way. "Look, Sean, here's what I can do for you: I can get you what belongs to you, including those IOUs, and I can take the Celeste Chandler heat off both of us by turning it on the guy who killed her."

"And what do I do for you?"

"Work on a guy a little. Maybe knock over a safe or two." McBride sighed. "That's one of the reasons I'm willing to forget how much I hate your guts. I'm a stranger in this goddam town. I don't even know where I can find a good pete man."

"A sad state," O'Hara said. After a moment he said, "Who killed her?"

"Sebastian."

"Why?"

"If I knew that would I need you?" McBride demanded. "Maybe I can guess, but that's no good. Some friends of mine down in the Federal Building wouldn't play a hunch as strong as this has got to be played. They've got to be gentlemen at all costs."

There was a brief silence before O'Hara said, "Your word that this is not just a build-up to take a pot shot at me in return for what happened out here?"

"I told you, didn't I?" McBride began to breathe a little angrily through his nose. "You play rough and I don't like it, but in your place I might have done the same thing." He thought about that for a moment. "Fact is, I'm going to try it out on this guy Sebastian, only I can't do it alone." He fumbled a crumpled cigarette from the pocket of Sigmund Loeb's overcoat and got it alight. "Make up your mind, Sean. Are you in or out?"

"In," O'Hara decided.

"And no bushwhacking?"

"No bushwhacking."

"All right," McBride said. He gave O'Hara a couple of addresses. "In half an hour I want both of those places staked out. I'm going to try to toll him into his apartment, but he might decide to go to the consulate instead. Tell your boys to let him go in, not to let him come out." As an afterthought he added, "And if things get rough they can shoot anybody they see except me."

"What do you get out of this?"

"If I work it right," McBride said, "I'll make friends with some people who can help me out of another jam." He scowled at the black face of the telephone. "Nothing like having friends—or is there?" He hung up.

When presently he dropped another nickel and got the St. Mark his hand shook a little, for this was the ticklish part of the whole business. Delilah Chandler's voice came to him, clear and distinct and perfectly controlled. He hoped it would stay that way, because he knew with almost utter certainty that Sebastian was there with her. "Mrs. Chandler?"

"Yes, this is Mrs. Chandler."

"Is Cesar Romero there with you?"

A little impatience crept into her tone. "Who is this speaking, please?"

"Your old pal McBride." He waited for her to gasp or do something equally foolish, but when she did not he said, "That's the old spirit, baby. Never let anything surprise you."

"What do you want?"

McBride said, "You're going to have to be something of an actress, darling. He is there, isn't he?"

There was only the briefest of hesitations. Then she said, "Yes, I'm waiting for my husband to come home."

McBride began to speak very rapidly now. "I'm not supposed to know that he's there, understand? As far as I know you're alone. This is important, Mrs. Chandler. You are to say to him that I believe he killed Celeste; that I am going over to his apartment to search it for proof."

She was undeniably shaken. "You're crazy!"

"Even if he heard that, it's all right," McBride said. "It's what you would say even if you thought it." He made his voice carefully impersonal. "But you don't think it—not really—because you've suddenly remembered that you were not with him when you said you were. You lied. You told him you were afraid you'd be suspected because you'd exposed your jealousy to me, and he said all you had to do was say you were with him. You didn't realize that it was he who needed the alibi."

She must have recognized her danger then; must have known that if by the slightest sign she let Sebastian see she was impressed, she would inevitably travel the same road as Celeste. Under the circumstances her laugh was an admirable thing. "You're being utterly ridiculous!" She disconnected.

"Good girl," McBride said under his breath. Again he called the St. Mark and this time got hold of the house dick. "You might keep an eye on the Chandler suite for the next few minutes. Just see that Mrs. Chandler is all right when her company leaves." Rather pleased with himself he emerged from the smoke-filled booth. It was like coming out of the steam cabinet in a Swedish massage parlor.

20

THE APARTMENT HAD an air of good living and sophistication about it, and if some of the more intimate touches were on the warmish, sybaritic side this could have been put down to Sebastian's Latin blood. There were some good etchings. It occurred to McBride's lewd mind that the etching gag was wearing a trifle thin and he wondered why some of these so-called eligible bachelors didn't switch to, say, ceramics. Behind him, the hall door did not exactly yawn wide, but a strong breath could have pushed it open and he had jammed the lock with a whittled match so that it would stay that way. He had had a little trouble with the lock, for it had turned out to be a special job not yet in general use. The lock encouraged him in the belief that he had come to the right place. He had finally outwitted it by prying loose a strip of door-stop and working directly on the tongue. The strip of molding still lay in the hall, mute evidence of the stupidity of the intruder.

McBride wanted Sebastian to think him more stupid than he actually was. He moved about the apartment, lights going full blast, in plain sight of the windows, deliberately creating an appearance of havoc without wrecking a thing. It was only by accident that he found the floor-safe beneath a modernistic radio-phonograph combination that looked as though it might contain liquor.

He was apparently fascinated by his newest discovery when behind him Sebastian's voice said pleasantly, "Hello, there!" McBride gave a realistic start. Sebastian said, "No sudden moves, please, Mr. McBride. You may turn around if you like."

McBride turned around. The side pockets of Sigmund Loeb's overcoat bulged with guns but McBride made no effort to use them. Angry-eyed he stared at Sebastian as though he, McBride, were the apartment's legal occupant and Sebastian the intruder. "So she told you!"

Sebastian held his gun almost daintily, as though not wishing to soil his hand. His eyes were intent and a little puzzled. "Yes, she told me." Without removing his gaze from McBride's face he backed carefully to one of the two divans framing the fireplace. Between the divans was a table on which was a telephone. "I think I shall call the police."

McBride shrugged. "Go ahead."

Sebastian's left hand caressed the phone cord. "On second thought, maybe I'd better wait a little while." The lean brown fist with the gun rested on a well-tailored knee. "Would you come about three steps toward me, please? No, no farther, Mr. McBride."

His eyes did not shift but McBride was conscious that a third presence had entered the room, possibly from the serving pantry. The whisper of feet on the carpet died directly behind him. "His guns, Manuelo," Sebastian said. "You will find one in either overcoat pocket."

McBride thought he had better struggle a little bit. When Manuelo's arms came around he pinned them to his sides with his elbows and kicked backward. Sebastian came off the divan with the lithe grace of a cat and hit McBride on the temple with the gun. A threatened second blow brought McBride's hands up to protect his face, thus releasing Manuelo who, snuffling like an eager puppy, emptied McBride's overcoat pockets with the adept ease of a magician. When McBride again kicked backward there was nobody there.

Sebastian returned to the divan. He was breathing a little quickly now and his eyes were unpleasant and hard. In Spanish he said, "You had better to look around outside, my little one. There is something here that is not right."

Manuelo's feet again whispered against the carpet. From the tail of his eye McBride saw that he was a small, dapper man suggestive of a brown ferret. Manuelo went out. It had all happened very quietly, with none of the sound and fury usually attendant upon such things. McBride wondered if perhaps Sean O'Hara had misunderstood him. He stood there in the middle of the floor, arms hanging loosely at his sides, and watched Sebastian's eyes. In them he could read nothing but that faint questioning, the wariness of an animal sensing something he does not understand.

Sebastian said, "It's an amusing thought that I should have killed Celeste, isn't it?"

"I practically laughed my head off," McBride said.

"But why tell Mrs. Chandler about it?"

McBride's weight came forward on the balls of his feet. "Because I expected her to tell you. Whether or not the alibi she gave you was a phoney she would have told you, but the way she did it was the deciding factor." He laughed a little. "You've got to give her credit. She was scared stiff but she put it over."

"I see," Sebastian said quietly. The thing that had puzzled him was gone from his eyes now. You could almost see the processes of an orderly mind at work. "Then you really believe I did it. Mrs. Chandler believes I did it."

"Yes."

"Why?"

McBride did not relax. He continued to watch Sebastian's eyes rather than the gun in Sebastian's lap. "Why do I believe it or why did you kill her?"

"Both."

"I don't know why you killed her," McBride admitted. "I can guess, but guesses don't count any more. All I know is that she was afraid of you, more afraid of you than she was of O'Hara or me." He shrugged his heavy shoulders. "Possibly something to do with what the FBI boys are looking for—the ones you thought were my assistants."

Sebastian rose to his feet. "Have you told anyone else of this—anyone besides Mrs. Chandler?"

"Oh, lots and lots of people," McBride said.

Sebastian's small frown of worry disappeared. "I don't believe you. If you had they would be here." After a moment in which he seemed to be listening for something, possibly Manuelo's return, he said, "No, I prefer to think that you would keep a good thing to yourself. I understand you private detectives are all—" He paused delicately.

"Scum?" McBride suggested.

Sebastian's manner said that this was his impression, though he was too polite to put it into words. "You have not yet told me how you arrived at the conclusion that my alibi was unsound."

"Oh, that," McBride said carelessly. "I just happened

to see you out at El Rancho Verdugo a short time after Celeste was killed. It occurred to me to wonder how you could have left so charming a lady as Mrs. Chandler—right in the middle of the evening, you might say—to come out alone to such a place." He eased the tension on his right leg a trifle. "Later on it occurred to me that Celeste's rather sketchy explanation of her first accident might not have convinced you; that you were, in fact, pretty worried over something that had caught up with her and might jeopardize you; that her crushed fingers were evidence that someone, possibly you, had forced the truth from her—her entanglement with O'Hara and so on—"

"So I killed her?"

"Yes," McBride said, "you did. You couldn't very well let her go on living afterward. She'd proven herself unstable and would be of no further use to you anyway." He shook his head in mild disparagement. "Naturally, because she had talked to you under pressure you wondered if perhaps she hadn't talked to O'Hara or me about you. That's what you came out there to find out." For just a moment his teeth shone whitely against the brown of his skin. "Cops have their uses, I guess. Orsatti's raid may have saved my life—who knows?"

"Who indeed," Sebastian agreed pleasantly. He looked at the exposed floor-safe. "I take it that you hoped to find proof of all this and then sell it back to me?" Quite suddenly he frowned. "No, that wouldn't account for baiting me here; for your call to Mrs. Chandler." He lifted the gun and pointed it directly at McBride. "I'm afraid I've underestimated you, my friend."

"Lots of people do," McBride said, and fell forward as

a tree falls, under Sebastian's first shot, and got the third gun, Orsatti's, out of his waistband and shot Sebastian's legs from under him.

When O'Hara and two of his men came in a moment later McBride had two guns, his own and Sebastian's, and stood looking with somber eyes at the man on the floor. "What happened to the Spick—the little one that went out of here a while ago?"

"We got him," O'Hara said. He went to the door as there were sounds of other doors opening along the hall outside. His magnificent presence, his almost pontifical manner stilled the clamor of a dozen voices. "Nothing to worry about," he said. "My friend was just demonstrating a new pistol for the army. It isn't quite perfected." His vast bulk blocked any possible view of the room behind him. Presently he nodded in definite dismissal. "Sorry to have disturbed you." He came in and closed the door and looked at McBride. "Well?"

McBride still stared down at Sebastian. His face felt as stiff as a board. "There isn't any other way," he said in a tight, unnatural voice. "Make him talk." A faint tremor ran through his frame. "I'm not very good at such things myself."

Sebastian was not suffering yet; shock and partial paralysis held him, but the full knowledge of the pain that was to come had not reached his brain. He lay half-propped against the radio-combination and he said, quite calmly, "I'll see you in hell first."

McBride drew a ragged breath. "That's probably what Celeste said, too—in the beginning."

At a nod from O'Hara one of the gunsels lit a cigarette.

The way he did it, the little final click as he snapped the lighter out, had a rather horrible significance. "What do we want to know, boss?"

From the windows, with his back carefully turned, McBride said, "The combination to the safe, first. After that, about him and Celeste Chandler." He opened a window and dragged deep gulps of cold night air into his lungs as the ugly stench of scorching flesh tainted the room.

After a while, after what seemed a terribly long while, he went to the telephone and called the Federal Building.

21

"I DON'T CARE," McBride said angrily. "I don't give one little good God damn; that's the way it is and that's the way it's got to be." He was addressing Mr. W. Patrick in Mr. W. Patrick's office, and you could see that he thought almost as little of W. Patrick as he did of Lieutenant Orsatti and Captain Wick, who stood over against the windows and regarded him without love. The time was ten-fifteen and over an hour had elapsed since the scene in Sebastian's apartment, a scene it was going to take McBride a long while to forget. He thought that presently he would find Butch Larsen and together they would go somewhere and get very drunk indeed.

Orsatti and Wick had but recently come in, and for their benefit Patrick repeated some of what had gone before. His voice was calm and unemotional; his brown eyes were not. It was obvious that he disliked McBride's shock-troop technique even more than McBride disliked the red tape of officialdom. "Mr. McBride suggests that I use my—that is, the government's influence with the local authorities to get him immunity for certain—ah—extra-legal acts." From a box on his desk he selected a brown paper cigarette and trimmed the ends with a small pair of scissors. "He not only wants immunity for himself, but for some friends of his whom he claims are more sinned against than sinning."

Captain Wick said nothing. Orsatti hurled a moth-eaten cigar to the floor in an access of rage. "Over my dead body! This guy runs around town knocking off people right and left; he's withheld all kinds of evidence from the law and made monkeys out of the whole department."

"But you mostly," McBride sneered.

Orsatti took a step towards him. "I want my gun!"

McBride got it out and laid it on the desk in front of Patrick. "Baby wants his stick of candy. He doesn't know that if I keep my mouth shut, Ballistics and some of his superiors might give him credit for knocking over Sebastian."

Captain Wick poked thoughtfully at his bristly red mustache. "I understand that it was Sebastian who killed the Chandler girl?"

"Not for publication," McBride said. He looked significantly at the brown man behind the desk. "Not unless Mr. W. Patrick needs less time to clean up the mess than I think he does. Either the whole business is hush-hush or it's going to be all dragged out in the open. Make up your mind."

A slow flush crept up around Patrick's ears. "I don't like your attitude, Mr. McBride."

"Nor I yours," McBride said nastily. "I won't be the fall-guy for a lot of stumble-bum coppers who think detection is picking on the first stranger they catch in town. If I have to show Chandler up for a sap, and by inference a lot of others of the same ilk, I'll do it." He spat disgustedly in the direction of the wastebasket. "Being a patriot, doing the work that your department should have done long ago, hasn't gotten me enough so far that I'm exactly crazy about it."

"You didn't do it because you were a patriot."

McBride scowled. "How do you know why I did it?"

"I can make a reasonably close guess," Patrick said, not without a trace of humor. "Your dickering right now almost proves it." He leaned forward and crushed out his brown-paper cigarette with meticulous care. "You detoured from your course long enough to solve one crime and presumably make me an accessory to whatever you have done in the past as well as what you intend to do in the future." He sighed. "Perhaps I should be grateful, but I'm not. Washington isn't going to be, either. If this thing ever comes out it's going to raise a squawk that will be heard from hell to breakfast. Not only the foreign diplomats but our own congressmen are going to yell about the American Gestapo."

"It doesn't have to come out," McBride said. He began pacing the floor with quick, angry strides. "Though an American Gestapo is goddam well what we need." He stopped and pointed a shaking finger at Patrick's nose. "The only way you can lick these guys is to fight as dirty as they do; forget the Marquis of Queensberry rules and bite and gouge and use a knee where it will do most good." He paused for breath. "You think I liked doing what I did? You think it didn't make me sick at my stomach? Christ, I had to keep telling myself every minute: 'This is what they'd do to you, baby. This is what they already have done. Remember Celeste Chandler's fingers?'" After a while he said more quietly, "It was lousy, but by God it worked."

"Yes," Patrick agreed, "it worked." He looked at Captain

Wick. "It seems that Celeste Chandler was not a Belgian refugee after all. She was planted as such, background and all, for the express purpose of being adopted into some prominent American family." He thought about that for a moment. "Hitler was already looking a long way ahead, you see, and as I recall it he has never been one to ignore the value of extreme youth. Celeste couldn't have been more than fifteen or sixteen at the time."

Wick said in a choked voice, "Children!"

Patrick nodded. "There's no way of telling how many more there are like her. It's just something else that we'll have to work on, that's all." He stared at McBride with eyes that had a little more warmth in them. "Perhaps you really have done us a favor—in addition to the particular circle in which Celeste and Sebastian moved." He leaned back in his chair and built a church and steeple out of his brown fingers. He looked a little like a thoughtful cleric. "We have Sebastian's records and we have his confession which, fortunately or unfortunately, depending on the point of view, Mr. McBride obtained by methods considered not quite cricket. We have Sebastian himself, and if there is no immediate exposure of that fact we'll soon have the rest of his associates."

He looked intently at Captain Wick. "That is one reason why we must avoid publicity. The other is perhaps less worthy, but as Mr. McBride has pointed out, anything that reflects discredit on our men in authority does more harm than good to the war effort." A somewhat wry smile touched his firm lips. "Mr. Chandler has been—again in McBride's words—a sap, and his naive intelligence has undoubtedly cost this country millions of dollars in damage similar to the fire last night over in the Oakland shipyard. In time he will be replaced. He will probably be made a Lieutenant-General."

Orsatti thrust out a truculent jaw. "So now we're asked not to prosecute a murderer! What happens to Sebastian? What's going to keep *him* from spouting off?"

"We'll take care of Sebastian," Patrick said. For a moment the muscles along his jaw line bulged. "I think Mr. Rodriguez Franz Sebastian is one of the things I'm going to make my personal business. If he lives, and I'm hoping he won't, I can guarantee he'll do no talking in public till long after what he has to say can affect the situation." His eyes rested approvingly on Captain Wick's red face. "Celeste Chandler just had an accident. You released that story yourself. I think it would be diplomatic if you stuck to it."

Wick cleared his throat noisily. "Suits me." He glared at McBride. "But I'm damned if I'll promise anything else until I know more than I do now. Who helped you on this? Where does the Chandler case tie into the Seversky kill— yes, and Slugs Foley's?"

"Up to a point," McBride said, "I'll tell you." He looked very hard at Orsatti's chin. "That stuff you found in the toilet belongs to a friend of mine; at least it belongs to him until the owners are ready to get it out of hock. So does the Adelphi and a few other odds and ends. He's got a right to it. He wants it back."

"Well, Jesus Christ!" Orsatti yelled. He appealed to Captain Wick. "Look, Skipper, it's as plain as the nose on your face he means Sean O'Hara. It's even plainer who knocked over O'Hara's joint down south. I'll leave it to you who killed Seversky and Slugs Foley."

"O'Hara."

"You're damned right it was O'Hara." Orsatti showed McBride a mouthful of tobacco-stained teeth. "And you want us to trade with you on that!"

McBride looked at W. Patrick. "You see what I'm up against. They haven't got anything on O'Hara. They haven't got anything on me—much. But they'll try to make something. Orsatti and his side-kick were all set to take me over the jumps in some two-bit flophouse once before and I wouldn't stand for it. I won't stand for it now." His eyes were muddy-looking. "I'm tired, and right at the moment my health is more important to me than some lousy politician's reputation."

Patrick addressed Wick. "Mr. McBride has a suggestion to make; one that does not seem so very unreasonable to me. He suggests that in return for some information he is prepared to divulge, Mr. O'Hara's rights be recognized and certain illegal acts of his own be expunged from the record."

Wick shut Orsatti up with an impatient gesture. "Wait a minute, let's get this straight." His eyes were bright and intent on McBride's face. "Give me the killer of Seversky and I'll make a deal."

"All right," McBride said. "Let's go see a little guy named McGillicuddy."

They all went over to the Trojan hotel, but they did not see Arthur McGillicuddy. Arthur had flown.

22

SOMEWHERE IN THE last half hour McBride had managed to get rid of Sigmund Loeb's overcoat, and though he had done considerable running around he was still cold. He stood with his back to the comfortable blaze in Susan's fireplace and sipped gratefully of the hot rum she had fixed for him. "So there I was," he said presently. "I'd given the cops a swell build-up only to lead 'em to an empty hole." He drained the mug and smacked his lips. "Orsatti swore I'd stalled on purpose."

Susan's eyes crinkled at the corners. "So what did you do?"

"What would you have done? I ran."

"Poor Arthur," Susan sighed. "I can hardly believe it."

"These little guys fool you sometimes," McBride said. "At least they nearly always do me." He came over and sat beside her on the divan and stretched his feet out toward the fire. "I couldn't imagine him lugging Seversky down that fire escape and into my room. He just didn't seem big enough for it."

Susan looked at him. "Are you sure he did?"

"Seversky's window was open," McBride said. "Mine was open." He leaned back and closed his eyes. "Besides, even though McGillicuddy had the run of the hotel, I can hardly see him wrestling a dead body through the halls." He shook his head. "No, it had to be the fire escape." After a while he said, "You know something, hon? It's these damned amateurs that always gum up the works. Give me a professional crook every time. You can figure them."

She shivered a little. "But you always win in the long run, don't you?"

He sat up straight. "What do you mean, win? I haven't got him, have I?" He stared intently at the palm of a hand. "I thought maybe—well, that you could give me a line on where he might be heading for."

There was a brief silence in which he could feel her drawing farther and farther away from him, not physically but spiritually. "No," she said presently. And after a moment: "I don't believe I should tell you, even if I did know, but I don't."

"He's a killer," McBride said.

She nodded soberly. "I know, but somehow it doesn't seem to make any difference in the way I feel about him." A strand of her copper-gold hair brushed McBride's cheek as she lay back in the crook of his arm. "What made you think of him in the first place?"

"I didn't," McBride said sourly. "Nor in the second place either." He looked at the fire. "Sure, he had the opportunity, and the stakes were big enough to attract a richer man than the manager of a flophouse like the Trojan,"—he blew out his breath, "when I found out what the stakes were." He got up and began moving restlessly about the room. "The trouble was, I didn't know, and even if I had I wouldn't have believed it. A convention and a strange hack driver and coincidence toss me right into the middle of something I'd been working on from a different angle. Then still another outsider has to stick his nose in." His smile was a trifle lopsided. "Up jump de ol' debbil."

"It must have been confusing," Susan agreed.

McBride kicked a hassock over to her feet and sat on it. "Celeste and O'Hara didn't help things any."

"Then it really was Celeste who hired Seversky and the others to rob O'Hara?"

McBride did not look at her. "Sure." He had let O'Hara believe this, too. His talk with the Deacon—the man's condition and his motive—had done something to McBride; he could not exactly say what. But he saw no sense in prolonging a hunt that could just as well end with someone it was impossible to hurt. McBride was finding it very convenient to have a lot of dead people lying around on whom he could saddle almost anything he wished. "Slugs Foley thought Celeste had crossed them up, that it was she who knocked off Severn, so Slugs paid her off for it."

Susan touched his head, a little diffidently at first, as though not quite sure of how he had taken her former withdrawal. "But Arthur?"

McBride made a bitter mouth. "Arthur was arrived at by the good old process of elimination—a stumble-bum method that takes a lot of time, but in a case like this the only one you can use." He laughed without humor. "You look up all the people who might have the stuff, make sure they haven't got it and that leaves you the guy that has." After a while he said, "Oh, there were things that pointed to him. He was on the spot; he'd had a chance to observe Seversky's goings and comings; he knew the kind of people he had under his roof, mostly crooks; it was possible that he was even spying on Seversky when Loeb called on him and made the offer for the Adelphi."

"But all these things you knew almost in the beginning!" Susan protested.

McBride shook his head. "I didn't know any of them. I had too many other people who were far better prospects." He scowled. "As far as the Hotel Trojan was concerned I was just a transient roomer whom somebody had saddled with a corpse. It didn't occur to me until later that I'd been stuck with the body *because* I was a transient; because Arthur had to stick *somebody* with it to remove any possible suspicion from himself, not only by the police, but by the regular tenants. Slugs Foley and Marge, for instance. If Seversky had been found in his own room they might have started wondering about their host McGillicuddy."

Susan was moved to a sort of unwilling admiration. "In a word, Arthur was smart."

"Oh, I don't know," McBride argued. He propped his head comfortably against her knees. "It must have been something of a shock to him to find out I wasn't the usual innocent bystander; that I was, in fact, a dick, and that I hadn't run away as no doubt he'd hoped I would." He laughed a little. "Remember? He fainted."

Susan pushed him away and stood up. "Yes, I remember."

"But you didn't faint," McBride said admiringly. "Not you. You took it all in your stride—just like you're taking it now."

She turned swiftly. "What do you mean by that?"

"Do I always have to mean something?" McBride complained. He, too, got up and helped himself to a cigarette from one of the fancy boxes scattered around. It was not particularly fresh. "What, no Chesterfields?"

"I'll get you some," Susan said. She moved toward the bedroom door.

"Wait a minute," McBride said. "A gun isn't going to do you any good. The police know almost as much as I do."

When she faced him she held her body straight and proud and her eyes were faintly scornful. "A gun, Mr. McBride? The police? I'm afraid I don't understand you."

"Sure you do," McBride said. He rolled the overly dry cigarette between his fingers. "Remember how carefully you emptied all the cigarette boxes last night—before I got here? Remember how you helped me smoke all mine up, so you could suggest that I go out after some?" His smile became a trifle wolfish. "Out in the fog where you knew Slugs Foley would be waiting for me?"

"I didn't!"

He went on inexorably. "So you didn't like the Chesterfields I brought you and you put the old ones back in their cute little boxes." He wiped his hands along the seams of his trousers. "Well, the cigarettes aren't important. They just go to show you how a lot of little things add up to a big one."

Susan had not moved. There was a little more color in her cheeks but her eyes remained clear and unafraid. "I'm supposed to be Arthur McGillicuddy's accomplice; is that it?"

"Rather his guiding star," McBride said. "An evil star. I think it fell on him." He began walking steadily toward her. "Remember how we talked about another woman I knew, and what I did to her? Well, this is going to be easier, because I don't love you and I never could have loved you. I'm in love with someone else."

She did not back away from him, not even when he was so close that the perfume of her was in his nostrils. She said, "That doesn't leave me a leg to stand on, does it?"

"I just thought we'd better get that part over with," McBride said calmly. He put himself between her and the bedroom door. "It must have been a game with you, I think. You didn't have to do it. Your people are all that you said they were." After a moment he said, "I don't know, maybe it's the war that's making us all just a trifle crazy."

Her sudden laugh sent a little shock through him. He watched her turn her back on him and move without hurry to the divan; watched with growing admiration as she sat and selected a cigarette and lit it. "Tell me all about it, darling." The assured smile on her lips was reflected in her eyes. "If it sounds even half reasonable I'll admit it."

"All right, I don't mind laying it out for you," he said. A slow flush crept up around his ears, for he was angry now. "McGillicuddy spotted the Seversky deal and told you about it. Maybe you didn't intend to kill anybody; maybe you just wanted a look." He drew a slow breath. "Anyway, you and Arthur were in Seversky's room when he came back unexpectedly and caught you. It didn't occur to me until later that what McGillicuddy couldn't do by himself, what you alone couldn't have done, the two of you could have done together. In the first place, Seversky wouldn't have let Arthur get behind him, so it was you who used the knife." He showed her his teeth in what was probably meant for a smile but was nothing but a grimace. "How'd it feel, baby?"

A shiver ran through her at that. Her smile became a trifle fixed. "And I once thought I might love you!"

He shrugged. "This is a brutal business." Presently he went on as though there had been no interruption. "Remember what you did afterward-when you found out I wasn't going to get panicked and run away? You sent me up after the Foleys." He laughed harshly. "Maybe you hoped I'd get them, or they'd get me and it would all turn into an unsolved mystery about where the stuff went."

Susan flipped her cigarette into the fire. "The policeman sent you."

McBride shook his head. "It was you who suggested the scream had originated in the Foleys' room." The backs of his legs ached and he would have liked to sit down but he would not. "So then you found out I was a dick and it worried you. You found out I was working on the Adelphi and that worried you even more. And McGillicuddy was a weak sister you had to keep bolstering up every minute." He stared at her with eyes that were suddenly bright and intent. "If I had been in your shoes I'd have gone crazy."

"You are crazy," Susan said calmly.

"No."

She stood up and put her back to the fire. "Then prove it, please. I've had a rather trying day."

"And you're not kidding there, either," McBride said. "Imagine having McGillicuddy to contend with! It wasn't enough that he had to be a weak sister; he had to be jealous, too. I'll bet you could have killed him when you learned he'd come to frighten me out of town; and still later had taken the risk of entering my rooms in order to plant some of the stuff." He admired her elaborately. "In fact you did kill him."

Susan widened her eyes. "Did I, Mr. McBride? How too, too dreadful of me! I think, as you suggest, I must have been quite mad."

"You yourself told me you were going to have a word with him," McBride said. "Remember? And Marge told me—yes, I had a guy named Butch waiting outside Siggy Loeb's house in case Marge should show up like the Deacon did. I was just out there and talked to her, and convinced her that if she and the Deacon just forgot the whole thing it might be a good idea." He smiled, this time not unpleasantly. "So she told me how she and Foley found out where I was dining last evening. Besides me, you were the only one who should have known that, Susan. You told McGillicuddy, so that if he happened to have any inquiries for me—"

For the first time Susan's eyes were a little frightened. "I don't believe you!"

"And the alibi you gave me with the cops," McBride said. "Maybe that was supposed to make me grateful in case everything else failed. Maybe it was just to get me out on the streets where you could have someone take another crack at me. You remembered what I told you about that other woman, didn't you, Susan? You knew I'd never give up till you had me six feet under, or as crazy about you as McGillicuddy was." He sighed. "What did you do with him, darling?"

Her breasts rose and fell unevenly. "I don't know what you're talking about!"

"Sure you do," McBride said. "Arthur was becoming a

terrific menace to you. He might crack wide open at any time. In fact you've known all along that I've more or less had my eye on him as a possibility. I suggested that you quiz him, remember? And I told you it might have been he who planted the stuff in my room." He stretched his arms high above his head and stood that way for a moment. "So you thought Arthur had better turn up missing. The only trouble with that was that Arthur wouldn't do it willingly. So you killed him."

Susan masked a small yawn with tapping fingers. "You'll need a body to prove that, you know."

McBride nodded. "The cops are looking for your car now." He watched her sway like a straight young sapling in the wind. "He'll almost have to be in your car, because you haven't had time to get rid of him so permanently that he'd never be found. You couldn't just leave him lying in a ditch somewhere. He was supposed to have run away with all the pretties, remember?"

She was suddenly and horribly afraid. "If I tell you where they are will you let me go?"

"No."

"I'm going anyway," she said. With incredible swiftness she bent and got the fire tongs and hurled them at his head. Flying feet carried her to the hall door and through it and along the hall to the stairs. Captain Wick and Lieutenant Orsatti, ascending, saw her coming at them. Her scream was still in the air when two quick shots put an end to it.

ENTERING THE ST. Mark an hour or so later McBride discovered Miss Kay Ford making a very lovely picture in a tall chair completely surrounded by luggage, some of which was obviously not her own. She was in caracul. All of the men in the lounge and not a few of the women were terribly conscious of her. McBride regarded her with acute dislike. "You again!" He looked at the pile of luggage. "I suppose Rourke couldn't get away from you. Where is he?"

"Out combing the various jails." Eyes so deeply blue they

were almost purple considered his somewhat disreputable appearance. "You look terrible."

"I feel terrible," McBride said.

"Did you know there was a policeman in your rooms?"

He nodded gloomily. "I thought there might be. I've had 'em practically sleeping with me ever since I hit this town."

"That must have been an annoyance to the handsome bookkeeper," Miss Ford said. A beautifully gloved hand indicated the briefcase under his arm. "Is she by any chance in there?"

McBride said carefully, "Please, hon, not now. Some other time." The white of strain showed along the muscles of his jaw line and his eyes were muddy. He pulled up another chair and sat in it with the briefcase between his knees. "All right, I'll give it to you fast and then I want to go somewhere and get stinking drunk." He drew her a swift stark picture, hitting only the highlights and without flourishes. "Besides the jewels O'Hara has got a hundred grand's worth of IOU's in here." He patted the leather between his knees. "He couldn't collect unless he produced—the kind of people he plays with wouldn't pay off if they even knew he'd lost them." He stood up. "Tell Rourke, will you?"

She too came to her feet. "Where are you going?"

"I just thought of something," he said. "I think I'll try to talk O'Hara out of the ten grand he loaned Celeste on the Adelphi." With apparently renewed vigor he bent and kissed her on the mouth right in plain sight of everybody. "He ought to be willing to do a little thing like that for a friend, oughtn't he?"

Her eyes were suddenly furious. "A friend!"

"Well, he is," McBride insisted. He seized her arm and led her toward the nearest bar. "All you've got to do to make friends is let 'em boot you around and maybe kick your teeth in a little and then do 'em a favor."

"I see," Miss Ford said dryly. "I take it then that you haven't an enemy in the world?"

"Well, maybe a few," McBride conceded. They came into the Coral Room and he thumped the bar loudly to attract a bartender's attention. "But honestly, hon, don't I meet the damnedest people?"

MOTIVATION IN MYSTERY FICTION

I HAVE BEEN writing for some ten or twelve years, undoubtedly the longest job I ever had. Before that, and not to be unique among writers, I was a little of everything—from soda squirt to "Big Business," with way stops such as section hand, private detective and art director in the movies. Out of all of which I've managed to salvage nothing but a reasonable understanding of human nature and its motivations. And there, in a nutshell, is the reason for what small success I have had as a writer. Neither consciously nor unconsciously have I ever permitted one of my characters to do a single thing which did not have a *logical, airtight motive:* a motive completely understandable to anyone. You will never find, for example, a character of mine jumping out of a second-story window when he could just as well walk down the stairs. On the other hand, if the stairs are blocked, or there are seven guys waiting out there to demolish our hero, then he has a perfectly good motive for using the window.

I use this sound motivation technique in even the little things. How much more important is it, then, to seat the story itself on a firm foundation! Why search around for obscure motives, or tricky motives, or downright silly motives, when the good, old-fashioned solid kind are right there before you? Why don't more writers ask themselves, "Well, what would I myself do in a given situation?" And then have the character do likewise!

With regard to weaving plausible yarns, if mine are plausible, analysis will show that said plausibility stems directly from this urge of mine to have my *characters* act like *people*. Maybe you, personally, don't know that kind of people; maybe their foibles and peculiarities are *exaggerated;* but *conceivably*, if placed in his or her position, you yourself would be very apt to act as he or she did.

As to creating suspense, well, just for fun, let's take one of my more profitable detective leads, a character named Rex McBride. (McBride has sold to both pulp and slick magazines, to the movies, to radio.) Here is a guy who is a heel in many ways. Yet he has a good point here and there. He loves and hates, lies and cheats, gets drunk and has a hangover, even as you and I. If someone kicks him in the stomach, it *hurts*. It hurts like nobody's business! And if someone does him an injury, he doesn't say, "That's okay, pal, I forgive you." You're darned right he doesn't. He gets sore about it, the same as anyone else in this day and age. But he doesn't just hate a man because that man has a crooked nose, or eats with his knife! He has a real, a *very* real, motive for doing the things he does. Lord, there we are, back to motive again! Well, can I help it? It's the motive that makes him do the things that create the suspense.

Let's analyze that: McBride is a private detective. He is hired to do a certain job. Now if there is one single thing about McBride that is admirable, it is his singleness of purpose. Maybe there is a point of honor involved; maybe his pride, his ego, or his reputation for getting results are responsible for the *drive* which forces him, and the reader, on. He has been hired to do a job and he's going to do it. Come hell or high water, he's going to do it.

And naturally, in a story, the "Hell and high water," or some very evil-minded guys and gals, are in there trying to stop him from accomplishing his purpose. The point is, they're in there *trying*, every minute, every page, just as hard as "McBride" himself is *trying*. He wants something. He wants it more than he wants anything in the world. And his antagonists are just as fiercely determined that he shan't have it. Why? Because they want to keep it themselves. Or they don't want to be hanged by the neck until they are dead. Or something. Ergo, if we don't have SUSPENSE now, we have a very reasonable facsimile.

Our hero is *always*, up to the very end, in *imminent danger of losing*, if not his life, at least that thing which he *prizes*, or is *trying desperately to get*.

As I see it, suspense is built on MENACE. This urgency both for and against does not only apply to a detective-mystery story. What matter if it be only a golf tournament? Our hero wants to win, doesn't he? And our villain, or villainess, simply isn't going to stand for his winning. No, sir! He wants to win, too. He wants to win, even if he has to resort to unsportsmanlike shenanigans, by golly. So is he a menace? You bet your sweet life he is. And does the *struggle* between the two opposing forces create SUSPENSE? Well, if the writer has done his job, it should.

Of course everybody knows all this. Every writers' magazine, every textbook on the subject of writing, is loaded down with it. But somehow, as it was in my own case, the necessary emphasis isn't there. That is all I hope to do, to emphasize this for others.

And while we're on *that* subject, my pet theme song is not going to work the same for everybody. For example, Lester Dent once wrote an article describing what he called his Master Fiction Plot. I, personally, got more out of two paragraphs of that than I had out of a dozen so-called textbooks. So I offered the article as pure gold (which it was) for the edification of other professionals; for that of the novices who sometimes come to me for advice; I even tried it out on my own son, who at that time also had lit'ry aspirations. And off-hand I'd say that less than ten per cent were affected by it as I was. Still, in this business, if you can help even ten per cent of your fellow travelers you aren't doing so badly.

Now for some other angles on the way I work. There has been an awful lot written about PLOT. Well, certainly a plot is necessary, unless you write for *Harper's, The Atlantic* or maybe *The New Yorker*. So what is a plot? Essentially, a plot may be fully and adequately described, as it has been, in that old chestnut: "Get your hero into trouble; get him out of it."

The main thing that is lacking there is that it doesn't mention *why* your hero gets into trouble. To me that is the vital essence of the whole thing. He gets into trouble *because* he is trying to do a certain thing. If I may say so, a *very* certain thing, and a thing that the normal, every-day human being (the reader) can easily and thoroughly understand without a diagram.

And the *trouble* develops *because* someone, or a whole

flock of someones, or maybe the elements, are doing their damndest to keep our hero from his goal.

Well! In the generally accepted sense I myself do not plot. By that I mean that I do not sit down and work out a detailed, blow-by-blow synopsis. I know many writers who do. I know many writers who, by the same token, rewrite their stories three and four times before the finished script goes out. And of these writers I know but one or two whose finished work, perfect in every last *technical* detail, has in it one single spark of life or real characterization. In other words, everything is there that the textbooks say ought to be there, but the stuff is as wooden and flavorless as some of the breakfast food you eat.

So what do I do? Well, first I get a character. I get a man that walks around, and breathes, and sometimes even spits on the carpet if he happens to feel like it. Sure, I romanticize him! I make him the kind of fellow I secretly would like to be; I make him do the things I'd like to do, if I had guts enough, or were smart enough. And next I find him something terribly important to accomplish; at least it's terribly important to *him*, once he gets started. And then, being a craftsman of sorts, I know I've got to get some other real red-blooded people, either to help him or hinder him. So I do that.

Well, the first thing you know, things pile up until the poor guy is in one Hell of a jam. Rarely do I bother with how I'm going to get him out—not at first. I'm too busy getting him in, and sweating with him, and getting kicked in the teeth. Then, along about the middle of the job—be it slick, pulp, or book—I go back and try to figure out *why* everybody did what he did. Sometimes this is pretty difficult. That is really when I start plotting. But believe me, if I can't find a good logical MOTIVE for each and every part, out that part comes.

I hope Albert Richard Wetjen will forgive me for this: It came to me second-hand from a mutual friend, as many of his words of wisdom have come: "The pulp story is concerned with what and how. The slick is concerned with WHY."

It is my contention that even the much-maligned pulp need not be *only* concerned with WHAT and HOW. The more of the why you can get into any story, pulp, slick, or literary, the better story it will be, and the better writer you will be, and if you want seriously to go on up—as most of us do— you will not say to yourself, "Nuts, this is meant for *Terrible Tales,* why bother!" You'll give a great deal of thought to the WHY, and keep putting it in there, even for *Terrible Tales,* and some day somebody is going to "discover" you, and lift you right out of that hole, same as they did C.S. Forester and his Captain Hornblower.

www.ingramcontent.com/pod-product-compliance
Lightning Source LLC
Chambersburg PA
CBHW070222030726
47505CB00006B/1784